ON MY OWN

D1260861

Also by Mitzi Dale

Round the Bend
The Sky's the Limit

ON MY OWN

Mitzi Dale

A Groundwood Book
Douglas & McIntyre
Toronto/Vancouver

Copyright © 1991 by Mitzi Dale

Groundwood Books/Douglas & McIntyre Ltd.
585 Bloor Street West
Toronto, Ontario M6G 1K5

Canadian Cataloguing in Publication Data

Dale, Mitzi, 1956–
   On my own

ISBN 0-88899-145-2

I. Title.

PS8557.A45305 1991   jC813'.54   C91-094532-2
PZ7.E35On 1991

Design by Michael Solomon
Cover art by Janet Wilson

ON MY OWN

ONE

"**L**ADIES ... FEELING STUCK IN THE KITCHEN? COOKING GOT YOU DOWN? CALL THE MUSICAL CHEF!" This was the moment of truth. With rubber bands, I'd attached a pot lid to each knee to make cymbals.

Kabang.

It worked! *Kabang, kabang.* That was easy. Balancing the wok lid on my head took skill. I hit it with the wok brush.

Ting.

So far so good. But I needed a rhythm section. I grabbed yet another lid and slapped the brush back and forth inside it.

Chicka-chicka, chicka-chicka.

"OKAY, LADIES, LET'S GET COOKIN'."

Chicka-chicka, chicka-chicka, chicka-chicka.

Kabang, kabang.

Ting!

"Kim?"

"Yeah?"

"Your father's trying to sleep!"

"Right. Nights afternoons days, nights afternoons days. OH, GOD, IF YOU HAVE ANY MERCY LEFT FOR YOUR LITTLE LAMB, DON'T EVER LET ME WORK AT STELCO. [ALL RIGHT, KIM.] WHEW. [DOFASCO FOR YOU.] GAK!

"Mum, lighten up. You're supposed to be my best audience."

"I'm not supposed to be your audience at all. I'm supposed to be your mother. And *you're* supposed to be making dinner tonight."

7

"I am making dinner. I'M THE ONE-MAN-MUSI-CAL-CHEF."

Chicka-chicka, chicka-chicka, ting!

"Here."

My mum handed me a pound of ground beef.

"OH, MY GOD. ITTH THE MATHTER'TH BRAINTH . . . you know, Gloria, you used to have a sense of humour."

"I used to have a daughter, too, not the spirit of Robin Williams."

"DING! GIVE THE LITTLE LADY A KEWPIE DOLL. Nice one, Glor."

I started to unwrap the meat. My mother was sighing. Actually sighing. One of those deep maternal numbers.

"YEW KNOW, MOTHEH DEAH, ONLY YESTADAY YEW WERE ACCUSIN' ME OF MOPIN'. WHY, AHM HAPPY NOW. CAN'T YEW BE HAPPEH, TOO? FIDDLE DEE DEE! OH, ASHLEY, ASHLEY! AH LOVE YOU. AH'VE ALWAYS LOVED YOU, ASHLEH."

She still hadn't cracked so much as a grin, but I didn't care. I wasn't about to let anything spoil my mood, not even a lack of appreciation for a fine routine. Wouldn't *she* feel awful some day, when my Scarlett O'Hara was famous?

I started singing like Snow White in the Disney movie — la la la la la la la — and I grabbed a couple of onions out of the fridge. I figured I'd make chili dogs. My brother Jamie always liked them. He called them sloppy doggies.

"What are you going to do with the prize money?"

Hm. My mother had never asked me what I was going to do with my money before. She knew I was saving it, but I'd never told her I was saving it to

8

run away and get started in *the biz*. I believe in keeping my parents on a need to know basis. Too much info and they get hysterical. Too little and they get suspicious. You've got to feed them just enough.

"I thought I'd donate it to the Funnybone Foundation."

"Kim . . ."

"No, seriously, haven't you heard of the work they do? God, it's amazing. You can leave your funnybone to medical science, and they can transplant it into the body of some humourless person. Think about it. It could change the world!"

My mother was just looking at me. I couldn't believe it. This was good stuff and she was just sitting there. Last night I'd won five hundred dollars at Yuk Yuks downtown and my own mother was just looking at me. I held the onions up to my eyes.

"Look, you're making me cry. SNIFF, SNIFF." Sheesh. "You know, Gloria," I started to tickle her, "you could use a funnybone transplant yourself today." She couldn't help smiling, but it was the tickling that did it, which is cheating. I started to chop the onions. The aroma of frying cow flesh was wafting through the kitchen.

"You haven't answered my question."

"You noticed that? DING! ANOTHER KEWPIE DOLL FOR THE LITTLE LADY." My mother did seem little to me now. I was five-ten and she was stuck way down there at five-four. Okay, okay, she was beautiful and had a perfect figure and creamy skin, but I had *height*.

"Have you thought about what you're going to do after school?" Mum asked.

9

"Oh, yeah." In fact, I'd thought about nothing else. There's no business like show business. What I hadn't told my mother, or anyone for that matter, was that "after school" was coming upon us like a freight train.

Grade eleven had been the worst year of my life, and I wasn't going back. I found out that my best friend Skye had been molested by her creep of a stepfather, then shipped off to a private school in France by her creep of a mother. Worst of all, they'd got to Brad and then Brad told everyone *I* was making up stories about *them*. My name was mud around Westdale High. Kimberly Mud Taylor.

"So what are you thinking about?"

"I was thinking about Skye."

"No, I mean, what are you thinking of doing?"

People were always asking Skye that question. I think it's because she had so much potential. She could do everything I could do plus math and chemistry and physics. But hardly anyone ever asked me what I was going to do.

"Are you trying to have a serious mother-daughter chat here?" I was opening a can of tomato goop to pour in with the ground cow.

"Yes."

"Hey, that's beautiful."

"Kimberly."

I stepped on the little pedal and threw the can into the garbage. I figured there was no time like the present.

"Mum. I'm going to be an actress."

"Oh, my God."

"What?"

"You can't be an actress."

"Why not?"

"You haven't done any acting . . ."

"I did Theatresports! And last night I won five hundred dollars for my portrayal of Amy the Typical Teen."

"That's not acting." She was right, but I still didn't like it.

"Mum, aren't you at all proud of me?"

"Of course I am, sweetie . . ."

"Well, then. I made five hundred dollars, for God's sake. If I did that every night — that's twenty-five hundred dollars a week!"

"Kim, when did they last have a contest like that?"

"They haven't." I stirred the sloppy doggie mix. "That was the first. But they're going to do it every year from now on."

"Then that's five hundred dollars a year. *If* you win."

"Look, once you've had a success like that, other things come your way. When I go to Toronto and say I won in Hamilton — "

"Wait a minute. What about Toronto?"

"Mum, I can't stay here. Nothing's happening in Hamilton. I've got to go to Toronto." There was a long silence as I started splitting open the hot dog buns and turning them upside down on the cookie tray.

"Kim. Are you thinking of not doing grade thirteen?"

Oh, great. My mum had this thing about grade thirteen. Probably because she went straight to secretarial school after grade twelve. How could I tell her I was not only not going to do thirteen but I wasn't going to do twelve either?

11

Some little demon made me tell her right then.

"I'm not going back this year."

"What?"

"I've been saving my money since I was fifteen. I'm going to Toronto."

"You can't quit school!"

"I THINK I CAN, I THINK I CAN. I KNOW I CAN, I KNOW I CAN." I guess I was hoping if I made myself obnoxious enough, she'd pay me to leave.

"You're too young."

"Priscilla Presley married Elvis at seventeen. Cher moved in with Sonny at sixteen, and when Teen Angel was my age . . . he was dead!"

"How do you think you'll support yourself?"

"Drugs."

My poor mother. Her funnybone failed her completely then, and she grabbed me by the shoulders and screeched, "Be serious, dammit!" This threw me for a moment. She was small but tough, my mother.

"Hey, hey, hey, girls." My dad was standing in the doorway in his pyjama bottoms.

"You've woken up your father!" *Me? She was the one who was screeching.*

"I've been awake awhile."

"You heard what she said then?"

"I heard."

"Well, do something."

"What am I supposed to do?"

"Knock some sense into her." My mum started shaking my shoulders again, and my dad stepped in between us.

"C'mon, c'mon, girls."

I went into a little boxer's dance, jabbing at the air.

12

"LEMME AT 'ER, MUGSY." No one laughed.

"Gloria, sit down, have some coffee." He poured her a cup. "Kimberly, go outside, walk around the block, count to a thousand something, come back in."

I went out and walked around a bit. I saw my old friends in front of Dundurn Liquor Store. I figured if I didn't make it, I'd beg. But I couldn't imagine not making it. And it didn't matter what my mum said, I wasn't going back to Westdale. I hated it. I figured once she saw how happy I was, she'd know it was the right thing. And how good I was! She and Dad never once went to Theatre-sports. I wasn't exactly the Star there — Skye was always the Star — but I'd had some hot nights. And Yuk Yuks! The triumph of my life and no one was there to see it. Sheesh.

When I went back home my parents were holding hands across the table and drinking coffee. My mother had been crying. Dad did the talking. I stood up and leaned against the sink trying to look twenty-five.

"Okay, Kim, listen up. You get a year." I started to protest. "I said listen. You get a year, a thousand dollars up front and you can come home any time you want to eat and sleep. Your room'll be here." I was adding up my savings in my head. "You listening?" I nodded. "You get a year to get this out of your system. But, after that year, no help from us." Long pause. "Unless you come home and finish high school. You'll be eighteen then, you'll be on your own, no help from us." He was really driving home the "no help from us" point, but all I could think of was a year on my

13

own and a thousand dollars. I'd never expected any help from anyone. This was a bonus.

My mother started to cry. I felt sorry for her, and I gave her a big hug, but I just couldn't be sad.

This was just what I wanted!

TWO

ONCE a decision like that's been made, you get rolling on it. I quit my job at Baskin-Robbins and figured I'd start looking for a place to stay. Things were a little strained between Mum and me, but she lived. It's funny. Kathy always used to say, "Mum'll die if she sees you doing that," or "Tell Mum that and she'll die." Well, I hit her between the eyes with quitting school and she didn't die.

My brother Ron helped me find a place. He was working full time at Stelco and thinking of marrying his girlfriend. Driving to Toronto, I thought how different we were. He was only three years older than me and already he was planning to get locked in for life.

We drove all over the place looking for rooms. Most of them were outrageously expensive and already snapped up by the university students anyway. I was like a tourist taking everything in. We were driving along Bloor Street, thinking of grabbing something to eat, when I saw a tiny sign in a laundromat. ROOM FOR RENT – INQUIRE WITHIN.

Ron pulled over and I went inside. It was a grubby laundromat with a door at the other end. I knocked on the door and after awhile it was opened by a man with an enormous belly hanging out over his belt.

"Yeah?" He was just wearing a vest and shorts. It was a very hot day.

"I'm interested in the room for rent?" He coughed and reached inside the door and grabbed the keys. I followed him up some narrow stairs to the first floor. A stove was right in the middle of the hall.

"You share that with two other guys." Gulp. It looked awfully greasy. "And the bathroom," he said, throwing open a door off the hallway. The bathroom was painted a ghastly pink, the ghastliness of which was somewhat softened by layers of dust and grease. The bathtub had a ring around it. The sink was small and had rust stains in it.

He turned the key in the door to the room nearest the bathroom and opened it.

"It comes furnished," he said. The room was ghastly green with a twin-sized bed with a mattress, no sheets, a small dresser and an end table and chair. The chair looked like it'd been stolen from an old dentist's office. It was green vinyl. There was a tiny little sink in one corner, complete with rust stains, and a window that looked out onto a brick wall.

The room was three hundred per month.

"I'll take it," I said to my new landlord. I had to hand over the first and last month's rent. Wow. The thousand from my parents was slipping away already.

"You're going to live there?" Ron was astounded when I came back to the car. "Mum'll die." When I told him what I was paying, *he* nearly died. He only paid twenty-five more for a big one bedroom apartment in someone's house in Hamilton, and he got his own bathroom. I have to confess, I was shocked, but I was so optimistic I figured I'd clean up my room and decorate it and it would be fine. I also figured I'd get a part in a show, meet a couple of nice girls and we'd move into a

16

penthouse apartment together and share expenses and blowdryers.

Ha.

My first night in my new place was very scary. I'd brought some sheets from home and some clothes, but otherwise there was nothing comforting. Just me alone in a dirty, hot, nasty little room. The other guys I shared with, it turned out, were hardly ever there. They'd come in around three or four in the morning, send the plumbing into convulsions, then crash into bed.

It seemed all I did that first week was spend money. I bought myself a one burner plug-in stove so I could heat up food in my room and not have to use the stove in the hall. My mum gave me a couple of old pots. I also took a huge plastic mixing bowl from home which I planned to use for sponge baths since the bathroom gave me the heaves. It turned out that only cold water came out of my little taps, so I would boil water on the burner and add it to the cold. Going to the bathroom was the worst part. I'd wait and wait and wait until it was go or burst.

I spent lots of money on cleaning stuff the week my parents were coming to visit. I bought sponges and cleanser and oven-cleaner and window cleaner. I decided to start with my room and leave the bathroom for last since it could be ruined at any time by one of the other tenants. When I wiped a sponge over the windowsill, the paint came off in big chips along with the thick dirt. But I kept scrubbing. I could hear my mother's voice saying, "Don't be ashamed of shabby as long as it's clean." I figured the window would have to be done once a week because it looked out on a narrow dirty alley that smelled awful on garbage night. I had to keep it open, though, because it was so hot.

So I cleaned the window. I washed the walls and even the ceiling. I did all this in my sponge bath bowl which got dark grey after a couple of wipes and had to be constantly emptied and refilled. My hands were raw and red, so I forked over for rubber gloves and hand cream. The floor was an awful linoleum that even after three washings didn't look clean, and each time I washed it some big bits chipped off.

After around three days the place smelled clean. My parents were coming the next day. I sprayed the inside of the oven with oven cleaner. I could not believe the gunge caked on that oven. I degreased the top of it with cleanser as much as I could, but there were lots of permanent stains. Permadirt.

The bathroom almost did me in. I actually started crying while I cleaned the bathroom. It was just filthy, and I think if one of the other tenants had appeared at that time I would have killed him. Every swipe of the sponge turned up hair mingled with dust and petrified bugs. *Who wouldn't be petrified living in that bathroom?* I took down the wispy little muslin curtains from the small window and put them in the tub. The water turned black. Of course, all that was holding those things together was dirt, so when I put them back up they were even more wispy. It turned out they were yellow curtains.

I was exhausted. Oh, for the beautiful little tub in Chatham Street! I spent a day on the bathroom and stove. Thank heaven it started to rain and took away some of the terrible heat.

Back in my room, I pinned a poster over a grease spot on the wall just above the bed where someone had obviously leaned his head. More Permadirt. It wasn't a showplace, but it was clean. Out I went again to get some cookies to give my folks with their coffee. More money spent.

My mum and I sat on the bed and my dad had the chair. I could tell they thought it was a hole but I resisted the urge to tell them how it had been a few days before. I joked about how great it was to live over a laundry. You could do a load at any hour, but that scared my mother and she made me promise not to do laundry after dark. The fact is, when the machines were going it was plain noisy and hot.

Ron hadn't told them how much I was paying, good guy, so when they asked I knocked a hundred off and they still thought it sounded like too much. My mum seemed on the verge of tears for the whole visit, so I only half noticed that my dad had his measuring tape out. When they left, my mum slipped me a twenty quietly and I confess I didn't bother to tell her Dad had done the same. Forty dollars wouldn't last me very long anyway.

The next week they turned up again, and the reason for the measuring tape was revealed. Mum had made some little curtains for my window, and they brought some paint and one of those big oval rugs you can get at Woolworth's. I have to hand it to them — they didn't force little prints and pink material on me. The curtains were sort of prehistoric stickmen on a white background and with the leftover fabric Mum had made me a pair of shorts. How many people have shorts to match their curtains?

My dad put in a thick doweling rod that went the whole width of my little room at one end, which turned out to be the greatest thing. I basically was living in a walk-in closet. We painted the walls and ceiling white, and they even bought a small can of black paint for me to do with as I pleased. I think they meant some sort of solid black border, but when they left I put a big Z for Zorro on one wall and saved the rest, figuring it would be fun to have people sign my wall. Then when I became famous and they made a shrine out of my apartment, there'd be all these names on my wall. Tourists would come from all over just to see the wall. Millions of homes would be having slide shows. *Click.* HERE'S GWEN AND THE KIDS BESIDE THE WALL. *Click.* HERE I AM BESIDE THE FAMOUS STICKMAN CURTAINS. They'd come by busload, and no one would leave unmoved.

THREE

I WAS rapidly running out of funds. Before I knew it, it was time to fork over another month's rent. I'd spent three years scrimping and saving and checking every payphone and now it was just flying out of my hands. Every time I stuck my head out the door it cost me ten bucks, and I still didn't have a job or an agent. Clearly, before getting an agent, I had to get a job and build up the bank book. I figured since New York actors worked in restaurants, Toronto actors probably did, too. Then you could practise entertaining your customers. The problem is, in New York everyone knows everyone's really an actor. In Toronto they were very suspicious.

"You wanna be an actress, right?" This was from a woman who hadn't even read my application. She just looked me up and down, saw that I was dressed all in black and had me typed. Like a fool I answered "yes" to this question. I answered yes a couple of times before I realized that this was why I wasn't getting any work. I soon learned to lie. NO, I'VE ALWAYS DREAMED OF SERVING REALLY FINE FOOD AND I THINK WORKING HERE AT HARVEY'S COULD BE A BEAUTIFUL THING.

By saying no, I got to a second interview. The second interview took place in the bar section of the restaurant. The restaurant was full of low-hanging lamps and maroon-coloured booths. My interviewer was a short man with a great deal of chest hair, who seemed bored to tears by life.

The job was a pretty big job. Cook's Helper. So I impressed him with my knowledge of chili dogs.

"Right," he said, chewing his lip. "See, basically this is a pickup place for professionals in the twenty-seven and up range. We know why they're here, they know why they're here, and we try to make them comfortable."

Oh, gosh. The colour drained from my freckled face. I don't know why he had to go and say that to me, since as cook's helper I'd be in the kitchen, not out front making anyone comfortable. It was probably one of the lines he used to separate the tough from the timid. It worked. I smiled weakly and had nothing to say. The interview kind of petered out, and Chest Hair said he'd keep me on file. I left.

It was good to get out in the bright sunlight. The Spaghetti Factory caught my eye. I didn't have an interview, but surely they'd need help.

"Hi, my name's Kimberly Taylor. Are you hiring at the moment?"

"Just a minute."

A tall well-dressed woman came back.

"Kimberly?"

"Yes."

"Can you start immediately?"

"Sure."

"Good. Follow me." She started to walk along the red carpet.

"You mean right now?"

She stopped and looked at me.

"I said immediately. Is that a problem?"

"No, no. I can start right away."

She started walking again, past the carousel horses and the choo-choo, into the kitchen. The

22

woman introduced me to everyone, but the only name I remembered right away was Silvy. Silvy had pink hair and she looked about my age. She was a dishwasher and my job was clearing tables, so we saw a lot of each other.

"You're an actress, right?" she said.

"No."

"C'mon. Everyone here is. I am."

"Really?"

"Sure. We all lied, too." She smiled at me. She had a ton of eye makeup on and a T-shirt with her own face done in blue glitter. I liked it. I liked her.

"Why don't they like actors?" I asked her in a whisper.

"They don't want you missing work for auditions," she said. "They want you to make spaghetti your life."

The woman came back with an apron for me and a tax form to fill out. I could hardly believe my luck. I had a job and a potential friend. Life was beautiful.

FOUR

SILVY was the first person to sign my wall. She
signed it Silvy X. That was her stage name. Her
real name was Silvia Donaldson. She tried to get
me to change my name to Flame because of the
hair, but I liked the idea of becoming famous with
my own name. Then everyone would know it was
me. It would be nice for my parents. Mum could
go into Jackson Square and people would point
and say, "That's Kimberly Taylor's mother!" But
best of all, everyone from Ryerson and Westdale
who thought I was a dork would be green with
envy. They'd be sitting in their living rooms with
their ten kids and their pot bellies and an ad for
my latest movie would come on. The little ones
would say, "Didn't you know her, Mum?" and
Mum would start to cry. Heh, heh, heh. How sweet
it is.

Silvy was my hero because she had already been
paid to act. She'd been an extra twice. She was in
"Narrow Margin" and "Bird on a Wire." We must
have watched "Narrow Margin" seventy times,
just to see Gene Hackman run past her. You'd
never have known it was her, but I was very impressed. I signed up with the same agency to be an
extra, too. About a month later I got a call and I
was so excited I almost wet myself. When I phoned
in sick, the boss was most unsympathetic.

"Kimberly, you've only been here a month. You
don't get time off."

"Ish not fer time off. I godda code."

"Jesus, I'm shorthanded as it is."

24

"Um, sorry, I cad hep it."

Silvy and I met for coffee at the Second Cup.

"What did you tell them?"

"I sed I ad a code."

"Oh, God," she laughed. "That's what I said."

"Oh, no."

"Never mind. I'll phone in sick tomorrow, too. It'll look better that way."

"Maybe I should?"

"No. I've been there three months. I'm almost indispensable."

We got the subway to the set. We had to be there by eight-thirty. I loved saying "the set." WHERE IS THE SET? WILL WE BE AT THE SET ON TIME? The set turned out to be Kensington Market, and I don't know why they bothered to hire extras because there were enough real people there as it was. We basically stood around for a couple of hours before anything happened. I was wearing a black tank top, my curtain shorts and black sneaks. I figured with flaming red hair and curtains on my bum I'd stand out. Wrong. I would have wondered, in fact, if we'd somehow got jostled along into a neighbourhood where no movie was being made if not for the odd snatches of revealing conversation.

"Valerie Bertinelli smiled at me once."

"I gave my apple to Barry Bostwick."

I was awed by these people, but Silvy wasn't.

"Gene Hackman is such a nice guy," she'd say. "What an actor." I knew for a fact that she hadn't actually spoken to him but it didn't occur to me that the others were probably stretching it, too. Silvy was such a pro. She'd brought a stick of sunblock and we just kept putting it on and putting it on. With my skin, standing around for hours in that sun, I'd have been a six-foot blister. To say nothing of how awkward it would be to explain to the boss that I god a burn id my bedrum.

For lunch we got a box with chicken and chips and salad in it. Free food! It was after noon and we hadn't done a thing. I think I'd drunk about ten cups of coffee, too, by lunchtime. This was a big mistake because it meant lining up for the johnny-on-the-spot which led to the incredible paranoia that I might be stuck in the john and miss my big scene.

I was wonderful in my scene. It involved milling about with sixty other people. Unless there was some incredible crane shot, there was no way my shorts were going to make it in the movies. Apparently Jaclyn Smith had walked among us. I was buzzed from the coffee and hot and my feet hurt, so even if she'd brushed my shoulder I probably wouldn't have known it. By the time they wrapped it up I figured we'd been standing for eight hours. This was harder than clearing tables. Then we had to stand in line forever for our money. They put a fifty-dollar bill in our hands. Fifty bucks! I was thrilled.

"Hey, Red, let's go blow some on Chinese food." Part of me thought I should save the fifty for my scrap book. I'd made a copy of my Yuk Yuks cheque and pasted it in, but my stomach was sticking to my back so I followed Silvy.

"So, what'd you think?"

"It was fabulous!"

"It was boring."

"Yeah, it was boring, but it was great!"

"After you do a few, you won't be so excited."

26

I followed her into this tiny little restaurant on Spadina.

"You ever had Chinese food?"

"Of course."

"No, you haven't. You're from Humbletown."

Silvy loved that word. She'd never even been to Hamilton and she had the idea it was this pokey little town.

"I know, I know," she'd say. "It's a city of over three hundred thousand. Wow."

I kicked my shoes off under the table and tried to surreptitiously rub my poor feet. Ooh. I was digging my thumbs into the ball of my left foot when the waiter came and lifted off the plastic table cloth. I thought my secret activities would be discovered but there were about ten more plastic cloths underneath.

"There's a neat trick," I said to Silvy. "My mum should know that one." My mum. I hadn't thought of my mum in ages. I'd been so caught up in the excitement of being on my own. Silvy saw it.

"Ah, a pang of homesickness, eh? Food will take your mind off that." She opened her menu. I opened mine, too.

"They don't have my favourite," I said.

"What's that?"

"Sweet 'n' sour chicken balls."

"Do not ever, ever let me hear you order anything with sahweet and sower sauce." She was looking at me in disgust. I closed my menu.

"You can order, Pink," I said, and I started to work on my right foot. I wasn't mad at her. She was impossible to be mad at anyway. She looked like a hooligan but she was the nicest person I'd ever met. Even when she made fun of me she

27

didn't do it meanly, and sometimes she made me feel amazing. Like when I told her about the Yuk Yuks thing. I hadn't told her about it before.

"So now you've made money from your craft," she said, pouring me some tea. "How's it feel?"

"Well, it's not really the first time."

"Really?"

"Yeah."

"I thought you said you'd never extra'd before."

"I haven't, but . . . well, it's not acting really, but I won some money in a contest." She put down her cup and her eyes widened.

"What? Tell me more."

"In Humbletown."

"It counts."

"Thanks."

"C'mon, don't keep me in suspense."

"There was this contest at Yuk Yuks and . . . I won."

"Ki-im! That's fantastic! You do standup?"

I'd never thought of it as "doing standup." I figured there was this skill out there called acting, and then there was this thing I did for laughs.

"Kim, you jerk, you should be going to Second City, you should go to the Riv, you should be bugging everyone to let you do a routine!"

"But I want to be an actress."

"Oh, excuse me, uh, wasn't that Robin Williams I just saw in a movie? And, oh, gosh, who are those guys?" She was clicking her fingers and pretending to think. "The McDougal Brothers. No, the McDonald Brothers . . ."

"The McKenzie Brothers."

"That's them! And the one with the nose . . ."

28

"Martin Short? He's from Humbletown, you know. So's Dave Thomas."

"Right. So how come you never put it together? This is your destiny, dipstick!"

"We never really think of those guys in Humbletown."

"I know, I know. It's all the yellow gunge you breathe. Zaps the grey matter." Our food came. I was getting kind of excited about Silvy's idea.

"I wouldn't know where to start."

"How did you get that wonderful job at the Spaghetti Factory?"

"I just walked in and asked." She was putting something in her rice bowl with her chopsticks.

"There you go."

"I wouldn't know where to start."

"You just start. I'll help you. I'll be your manager."

"Ten percent."

"Once you're famous."

"It's a deal. What is this?" My food kept slipping out of my chopsticks.

"Eggplant." I finally got some to my mouth.

"It's slimey."

"It's delicious." She leaned forward and fixed me with one of her Gazes. "You're going to be quite a project, Red. I'm here to expand your consciousness."

FIVE

DON'T think, just start. That's what my improv teacher was always saying. Back at work the next day I missed Silvy, but it was good she didn't come. My supervisor kept looking at me suspiciously, even though I'd worn no makeup and put baby oil on my hair to make it look greasy. I'd also rubbed Vaseline on my eyelids. I was prepared to snort pepper if I had to, to make myself sneeze, but constantly clearing my throat did the trick.

Some of the greatest acting of my life was done at the Spaghetti Factory.

When Silvy did come back we had our usual bizarre interrupted conversations because I had to keep moving and be seen to be keeping moving. I'd dump a trayload beside her and say something, then go clear a table and come back with another load and she'd say something back.

"What's the Riv, a club . . . ?"

"No, a restaurant on Queen Street, the Rivoli . . ."

"Why would they want a comic . . . ?"

"They do stuff . . . poetry . . . it's worth a try . . ."

"What if they say no . . . ?"

"What've you got to lose?"

All this might take place over an hour, because when I wasn't clearing I had to set tables. Silvy invited me back to her house that night.

When I hear the word "house" I automatically picture a mum and dad and bicycles on the front lawn. When I got to Silvy's house there was one bicycle, but it was a motorbike, and it wasn't on the lawn, it was in the front hall. There was no mum and dad but there were two girls and a guy. There were two more, apparently, but they were out that night.

"Mike, China, Lucy, this is Kim."

"Hi."

They all said hi. They were watching TV in the most awful living room I'd ever seen in my life. With two brothers and a sister I figured I'd grown up in a zoo, but this place took the cake. There were magazines and bottles and cans and huge Kentucky Fried Chicken buckets all over the place. It wasn't just messy, either. It was dirty. We went into the kitchen to get a drink and there were no clean glasses. When Silvy lifted a couple out of the sink, this slimey stuff like egg white dripped off them.

"I don't see why I should wash dishes here after washing dishes all day," she said loudly, but no one in the living room said anything. She squirted some soap in each of our glasses and cleaned them and grabbed a Coke from the almost empty fridge. There was a bunch of soy sauce packets in there but precious little else.

We went upstairs to her room. There were five bedrooms and an upstairs and downstairs bathroom. It would have been a neat house if it had been cleaned up and repainted. It was way bigger than my old house on Chatham Street, but it seemed smaller because it was really narrow and every available space was piled high with junk.

Silvy kicked the door shut and sat on her bed. It hadn't been made and the sheets were grey. Permadirt. My mum *would* have died if my sheets had been like that.

31

"Pretty neat, huh?" she said, handing me a Coke. The Coke was cold, but the glass was still warm from being washed.

"You guys own this place?"

"No way. We rent it."

"Where does the owner live?"

"Down the street."

I didn't say it, but I was wondering how the owner could stand having his house look like that. "What do you pay?"

"My share is three hundred."

"That's what my room is!"

"Yeah," she waved her Coke, "but I get a whole house."

Maybe it's because I'd already lived in a house with six people, or maybe it's because I was becoming antisocial, but I would not have traded my little room for that house for a million dollars. Besides, if I lived there I'd have spent my whole life cleaning.

"Do you have a comp? Photos?" she asked.

"Are you kidding?"

She got up and opened a drawer in her bureau and pulled out a sheet of paper and handed it to me. It had three pictures of Silvy on it and underneath her name, height, weight and eye colour, some of the things she'd done. She'd written in the last extra work we did in her own writing. At the bottom was the name of a talent agency. Stagewise.

"You choose three different pictures to show your range."

In each picture she had tons of makeup and a black leather mini. In two of them her mouth was open and in the third she was kind of scowling. I guess that was to show range. I couldn't imagine her getting anything but porn parts with those pictures, but I didn't say it.

"Have you got work with these?"

"I just got them. I'm going to do a massive distribution on Monday."

I wrote down the name of the agency and Silvy put her comp back in her drawer. If I had to do it, I had to do it. We got the phone book out and Silvy made up a list of places I should try for standup time, but first I had to get a comp. We agreed I'd go to her agency the first day I got off and then we'd get together for further plans. *My place next time.*

SIX

SILVY'D said I could use her name, but when I got to the agency the woman, Marlene, didn't know who she was.

"Silvy X. Pink hair?"

"Oh, Silvy!" she said with a big smile. "Great girl." But I didn't think she really remembered her. She took me into a little room and sat me on a stool and focussed a camera on me. My face flashed up on a TV screen. It was weird. My nose didn't look too enormous on TV.

"Okay, Kim, try not to look at the screen. That's right. Now, tell me, Kim, who's your favourite actress?"

"Katharine Hepburn."

"Oh, wow. Now I want you to pretend you're Katharine Hepburn for me."

Oh, great. If I'd known she was going to ask that, I'd have said Vivien Leigh. I didn't know whether to do the Hepburn of "Guess Who's Coming to Dinner" or the Hepburn of "Holiday." One old and one young. I did both and she didn't object. Then I had to do a pretend commercial for anything I felt like, and I did the Doublemint Twins. I thought that was incredibly clever of me because it would show I could sing, too. I was pretty pleased with myself.

"You have a nice voice, Kim."

"Thanks."

"You can wait outside and someone will see you shortly."

I sat in the waiting room which was fairly full.

There were mostly girls but the odd guy came in and there were quite a few kids with mothers. The walls were plastered with glossy pictures. A picture of Cher and Marlene caught my eye and I went closer to have a look. It wasn't Cher, though. It was a Cher lookalike, and not even a very great one. There were about ten pictures of looka-likes — Cher, Spock, the entire Royal Family. I noticed that Silvy's picture was nowhere in sight.

After about half an hour I was called into another room and a man in a blue suit gestured for me to sit beside his desk. He seemed to be chewing a tiny bit of gum in his back teeth. He was holding a sheet of paper which he put down on the desk in front of him. He started to nod and there was that slight chewing movement. He had this way of using his hands that bugged me. He put both middle fingers on the page in front of him, one at the top and one at the bottom, so that his other fingers were splayed like an airplane. He twisted the sheet to face me. It was a kind of chart with red dots stuck on it.

"Your test was excellent, Kim, excellent." I felt excited. He picked up a pen and started pointing to the chart.

Qualities Tested	Below Average	Average	Excellent	Career Option
Photogenic Ability			•	*good look*
Expression		•		*animated*
Voice Projection Inflection		•		*more inflication*
Confidence		•		*relaxed*
Take Direction		•		*attentive*
Film Possibility		•		*good*
Television			•	*yes*
Modelling			•	*print*

Should continue ___*with training*___ Advised not to continue _____

Tested by ___*Marlene*___

Approved _____

He read the congratulations blurb out loud, upside down. I felt like saying, "I can read and besides inflection is spelled wrong," but I was too flattered. Then he flipped the page and read Marlene's assessment.

"'Kim would be suited to older sister, best friend, high school and early college parts. Her age range is sixteen to twenty-four. Acceptance strongly recommended.' We're impressed, Kim. We're very impressed." I could have floated up to the ceiling.

"Now," he swivelled and brought out a blue binder, "twice a year we update our Promising

Faces book." He started flipping through the binder using those middle fingers. "Our photographer will be here all day tomorrow and I'd like to book you for a session. The picture of your choice will be used for Promising Faces and we'll give you our input if you want help choosing." I was unbelievably excited. It would mean calling in sick again, but that was okay. He pulled out another sheet of paper.

"If you want to sign up for that now . . ." He held a pen out to me. I looked at the sheet. I was signing for a photo session tomorrow and I'd have to pay six hundred dollars. Gulp. That was a lot of money. He saw me hesitate and chewed a little and leaned back in his chair. He looked a bit like Chest Hair then.

"What's the problem?"

"Six hundred dollars?" I said. He chewed his lip.

"Look, Kim, you got to spend money to make money in this business."

"Can I think about it?"

"The photographer is coming tomorrow."

I was about to sign, because I figured for six hundred dollars I was getting an awful lot. A composite, a photo session and the Promising Faces book.

"How many comps will I get?"

"What?"

"How many copies of my comp will I get?"

"Okay. The composite's a separate thing. We can do that anytime. Promising Faces is tomorrow."

"But I get it all for six hundred dollars?" He

was starting to look really bored, just like Chest Hair.

"Comps are very expensive, Kim, but for a one-shot deal of six hundred dollars, you get your picture in Promising Faces. Now, you want to be stuck with a thousand comps *you* have to get rid of, or do you want a professional like myself distributing this book," he held it up again, "to the people who are casting in this town?" I didn't like the sound of "getting rid of" the comps.

"My friend Silvy, with the pink hair?" He just looked at me and chewed a little. "Silvy got comps." He leaned forward.

"Look, Kim, between you and me, you've got real talent. I said it before, we're impressed. Now, if we put everyone in Promising Faces, what would be the point?"

This made sense, but I didn't like it. Silvy'd paid a lot of money for her comps. And I was sure they told her she had to have comps.

"So comps aren't important?" He was getting tired of me. I was too thick-headed about the biz.

"No one looks at them, 'cuz they're sent in by starstruck kids. But Promising Faces," he held up the blue binder again, "is sent to casting agents by a reputable talent agency. Stagewise." He put the binder down and put the pen in front of me. It was tempting.

Maybe it's because my mum's a legal secretary, but I felt I was being rushed to sign.

"I'd like to think about it."

"The photographer won't be here for another six months. In that time fifty major film companies from the States will be up here making movies." I'd already been in one of these movies. I couldn't imagine my face in a wallet-sized picture among hundreds of others getting singled out for a speaking part.

"They cast from these books?"

"Look, if you were a director and you wanted a lovely young woman with flaming red hair to play the older sister in your new sit com, wouldn't you want to make your life easier, flip through a book like Promising Faces," he held it up again, "and pick out five or so to audition?"

"The pictures are in black and white, though." He was getting really bored now.

"Listen, Kim. If you got the Look they want, you got the Look they want. Unless they see your picture, they'll never know you're out there. Now, you sign, and Marlene will book a session for you tomorrow." He looked like he was about to take a nap. I felt I'd taken too much of his time. But I just couldn't bring myself to sign. Six hundred dollars. Two months' rent for a little black-and-white picture on a page of about thirty pictures in a book with hundreds of pictures. You'd have to have Mickey Mouse ears or look like Skye to stand out in that book.

"Could I pay just a hundred now and pay you out of the money I make?"

"Look. As an artist, you should be able to pick and choose what you do. Say you get cast in a commercial for beer or something, and you're a teetotaler. You wouldn't want to do it, but to pay us, you'd have to do it. No, in order for our clients to have total artistic freedom, we insist on the money up front. It's more fair to you and it's more fair to us."

Artistic? I'd do anything! Why was this guy throwing in the artistic crap all of a sudden?

"I'll have to think about it," I said and stood up. He opened his hands wide and shrugged. I could feel his disappointment in me. When I walked back through the waiting room, Marlene wasn't there. She must have been videotaping someone else. I looked at the glossy pictures again and left.

In the room with the guy, I'd felt like he was trying to pitch me something worthless, but back out on the street I felt like I'd turned down a chance at stardom. I was a wreck. Why hadn't I signed up? What's six hundred bucks? I had no idea where to start, but an agency would help me.

Except, he didn't seem too helpful. The comment about getting rid of the comps really bugged me. Oh, well, Silvy was coming to my place for dinner and we could talk about it together. I figured I'd make my specialty, Crap Dinner with my own special touch — a hunk of cheese, grated and added to the pot with the sauce packet.

I was feeling depressed, but a guy playing saxophone on the corner perked me up, so I put fifty cents in his case. He reminded me of the couple who used to fiddle and sing outside Jackson Square Mall in Humbletown. He looked happier, though. I wished I'd learned to play guitar so I could stand on the corner and sing for my supper.

I could hear Kathy's voice in my ear. Mum would die.

SEVEN

SILVY turned up with a bottle of wine spritzer.
"How did you get that?"

"Lucy. She's nineteen. She's taking Anthro at U of T."

"How'd you meet all those guys?" I grated the cheese and Silvy poured us mugs of spritzer.

"I met Lucy in Germany and China out west. The rest just kind of turned up. Lachaim." We touched mugs and sipped. The spritzer was fizzy but I could taste the booze. We were always allowed wine with Christmas dinner at my house, and at Skye's sixteenth birthday I'd had champagne.

"When were you in Germany?"

"Two years ago. I bopped around a bit, met Lucy, we made each other homesick and so we came back and got the house. And here we are."

Silvy leaned against the foot of the bed and I leaned against the headboard and we ate our dinner from bowls. It wasn't long before we were talking about Stagewise.

"What's this Promising Faces? They didn't tell me about that. Are you going to do it?"

"No."

"No? You short of money?"

"It's not just that. He seemed awfully fishy."

"What do you mean?"

I didn't have the heart to tell her about getting rid of comps, or that he'd suggested she wasn't "special," but I told her everything else. She got up and grabbed her purse and pulled out an envelope

41

from Stagewise with her assessment on it. "I keep this on me to look at when I get depressed." I pulled mine out and we put them side by side. It was incredible. They were identical, right down to the placing of the dots on the line between good and excellent. Silvy's assessment was the same as mine, too, except it included an ability to play punks.

"At least they noticed the hair," she said. I thought she was going to cry. The tears were just sitting there ready to drop. "How could I have been so stupid?"

"How much did you pay?"

"All told? About fifteen hundred bucks. Damn!" She threw her assessment across the room. Then she looked at me.

"How come I was taken in and you weren't, Humbletown?"

"Listen, if not for the money, I'd have done it in a flash."

Silvy poured herself another spritzer.

"Well, what do we do now?" I asked.

"We get you into a club," she said.

"Oh, right, that should be easy." I wasn't even too sure I wanted to do it. Yuk Yuks had been a rush, but it wasn't what I wanted to do with my life. I wanted to make people cry at the movies, not laugh over their eighth beer at a club. Silvy was obsessed by the idea, though.

"Let's hear some of your routines."

"Nah."

"C'mon. How can I be your manager if you don't show me your stuff?" So I did my winning routine that I'd used in Yuk Yuks. Amy the Typical Teen.

Silvy sat through it all without laughing. She

chuckled a little when Amy tossed her baton. When I finished she just kind of looked at me. They'd gone wild at Yuk Yuks. Maybe it was the large crowd. Maybe it was the eighth beer.

"I don't know if that would go over here," Silvy said. "GLV's might not make Toronto people laugh."

"What's a GLV?"

"Good Little Virgin."

She must've seen the colour draining from my freckled face.

"Oh, my god. *You're* a GLV?"

"GTV. Tall." Silvy was shorter than me.

"No kidding. You're the only one I know."

"Well, gee, maybe we can sell tickets. Maybe that's how I'll get into the clubs! I'll tell people I'm a virgin and they'll go, OH, MY GOD, WAIT RIGHT THERE. And they'll go away and come back with three other people who won't believe it, either. And they'll throw a net over me and put me in a cage over the bar. And they'll put a sign out front — VIRGIN INSIDE. ADMISSION ONE DOLLAR. People will pour in and poke at me through my cage. I'll start out snapping at them, GRRR . . . but after awhile my spirit will be broken, and I'll just rock back and forth, picking my toes and singing, I AM SIXTEEN GOING ON SEVENTEEN. They can loan me to the Chinese in exchange for a panda. I've always wanted to travel."

Silvy was laughing.

"Hey, that's not bad."

"Thanks." I got some more Crap Dinner and plopped back against the headboard.

"And you sing?"

"Oh, yeah." I did my Sonny and Cher imitation. A few bars of "I Got You Babe."

"The baby boomers'll eat you up!"

"Or alive." Actually, I knew my Sonny and Cher imitation was good. Kathy was a Cher freak, so I had to listen to her for years when we shared a room.

Silvy was genuinely excited by the idea of being my manager. It seemed to get her mind off being taken by Stagewise. She made up a list of clubs and places I should go to get standup work.

"Look at it like getting a job," she said. "Which it is. You go to two places a day, minimum. And you let them hear you sing."

"Oh, yeah. That should be easy. I'll just go in singing. HOW DO YOU DO?/ MY NAME IS KIM/ I'M A COMEDIENNE/ ARE YOU HIRING?/ OH, NOT RIGHT NOW/ GIMME A CALL."

"You'd be remembered, anyway."

"Yeah, like, 'You know that redhead? Remember not to let her in again.' Or, 'That tall skinny kid with the nose? Remember not to call her.'"

"Your problem is, you're lacking in confidence."

This was true. At least, my confidence came and went on me. Sometimes I had tons, like the time I did my grade nine speech about adolescent boys, and sometimes I had none, like the time I got glued to the Theatresports bench leaving Skye to become the Star, which she did. Having the beautiful talented Skye Manning for my best friend was all part of my plan to get more confidence, but it hadn't always worked that way.

"Hello? Hello? Anybody home?" Silvy was

snapping her fingers in front of my face. "You were drifting."

"I was not."

"Yes, Orenz, you were. You were drifting."

Orenz! Orenz! She was a Lawrence of Arabia fan! We went back and forth doing bits from the movie.

"Of course it hurts. The trick is not minding that it hurts."

"Auda aboutai!"

"Thy mother mated with a scorpion."

"Nothing is written."

And then, together, the crazy war cry of a thousand Arabs on camelback.

"Awooawooawoo!"

We laughed so hard our stomachs ached. I was so happy. But it did remind me of the time Skye and I had gone to the all-night Peter O'Toole festival at the university. That was the first summer we were friends.

"Now what, Humbletown? Homesick again?"

"Friendsick." Maybe it was the spritzer, but I got a little weepy and told Silvy the whole Skye story. How I'd set my sights on getting her as a friend because I was a dork and didn't want to go to high school as part of the dork crowd. I even told her about Brad and how unreal he was.

"You liked this guy?"

"Oh, yeah."

"You still like this guy?" The fact is I did. Even though he had believed the lies about me, I still liked him. I couldn't help it. I told her all about Skye's house and her double doctor mother and rich stepfather Paul. And I told her what Paul had

45

done. I thought she might not believe me, but she did.

"Skye's at Le Lycée Canadien now," I said. They'd whipped her off to France after she tried to kill herself. "It's a private school."

"I know what it is," Silvy said. "I went there for a year."

"You're kidding," I said. "You know French?"

"Oui, et parce que j'ai une facilité avec les langues, je parle aussi italien et un peu d'allemand."

"Whatever it was, it sounded great!" Silvy laughed. Then something occurred to me. "Don't you have to be rich to send your kid to those schools?"

"I would think so."

"Then how come you live in . . ." I was going to say "a pigsty," but I caught myself, "in a house with five other kids and work at the Spaghetti Factory?"

"There's rich like your friend Skye, who takes it, and there's rich like your friend Silvy, who doesn't."

"Oh," I said. "Oh."

Silvy was the kind of person Skye wouldn't have thought much of. Pink hair, too much eye makeup, thick ankles. But she was on her own and not taking anything from anyone. She dressed in this strange-neat way, but designer names weren't anything to her. Skye could tell a Calvin Klein from a Ralph Lauren at forty paces. Or so she said. Silvy made a point of puking over designer names. She was okay. I liked her. Her only flaw was that she seemed to think if I lost my virginity I'd be a better comic.

"You'll make non-virgins nervous."

"Do I make you nervous?"

"No. But I'm different."

"How come?"

"Because. I can handle purity."

"Get out of here." I threw a pillow at her.

"Seriously. You can't be a really good comic, or any kind of actress, without losing your virginity. Think of it as a career move."

Career move? What would my mother think of that? Our heart-to-heart talk had consisted of graphic descriptions of sperm-meeting-egg, along with a booklet provided by Kathy. And she'd ended by saying, "There's more to love than sex. Don't be in a hurry."

"Don't be in a hurry," Silvy laughed. "That's great! Anyway, she was right in one way. It's a real let-down. That's why I think you should do it. Get it out of your system. Then you won't be in a sexual frenzy all the time just thinking about it."

"I'm not!"

"Sure you are. How many times a day do you think about it?"

"Hardly at all."

"C'mon."

"All the time."

"Aha!"

"But I'm not concentrating on it or anything. I'm just vaguely aware of it."

"Right. Vague, filmy little thoughts flow through your mind like Brad in the moonlight, Brad on the terrace, Brad on the beach. A button here, a button there, the Kiss. A flashforward now and then, but lots of flashbacks. To the buttons."

Oh, God, she was absolutely dead on. She knew she was by my expression.

"Well, it's not like that, sweetheart, so forget it. It's fast and messy."

"What if you're in love?"

"You or him?"

"Both of you."

"Very rare. Unknown in my experience but, perhaps for someone of your romantic nature . . ."

"Romantic? You think I'm romantic?" I'd always thought of myself as realistic and tough.

"Oh, yeah. Leaving Humbletown to make it in the Little Apple. Living all alone in this . . ." she looked around my room, "place with the curtains. You're a romantic all right, Red. Nooo doubt about it."

The love stuff was bothering me.

"My parents are still in love."

"Really? How do you know?"

"They're always kissing and hugging."

"Hm. Sounds like comfy-love. An old shoe kind of relationship, you know? No passion but lots of companionship. A nice way to sail into the sunset, but I'm not ready for the sunset yet."

Neither was I. Whenever I imagined myself with Brad, it was just like Silvy'd said. On the terrace. I never thought of us walking around the block hand in hand like my mum and dad. Oh, well, at seventeen I didn't think I really had to worry about this. My plan was to be making a living as an actress by twenty, then at twenty or twenty-one fall madly in love, get married but put off having kids till about twenty-seven or twenty-eight. In fact, I wasn't even sure I wanted kids. I'd probably have a bunch of nieces and nephews and I could be the wild aunt who flew in from London and Paris with fabulous gifts. I'd buy my mum and dad a nice house in West Hamilton or Dundas and my Oscars would start to pile up on the mantelpiece. My mother always wanted a fireplace.

Silvy clicked her fingers again.

"You're not concentrating. It's probably the spritzer."

"Cookies for dessert," I said, unfolding my legs. "You want coffee? It's instant."

"Yeah. Not a bad meal, Red. The extra cheese helped."

"Thanks."

"I mean, you're incredibly naive and you're a GTV, but what you lack in experience you make up for in common sense and domestic skills."

I plugged in my little kettle and put the cookies on a plate between us.

"Fig Newtons?" Silvy picked one up and looked at it. "Fig Newtons?"

"Yeah. Don't you like them?"

"I haven't had Fig Newtons since I was eight."

"They're best with milk."

"Oh, yeah, milk and Fig Newtons. I remember." We both looked at the kettle, then back at each other.

"It has to be ice cold, though," I said.

"Unplug that kettle," Silvy said, and she grabbed her bag and disappeared. She came back in about ten minutes with a large carton of homo milk. We polished off the whole carton and the whole package of Fig Newtons. We dunked. We slurped. It was an orgy. An eight-year-old orgy. Silvy was flat across the bed finishing her last little bite of Newton and her last sip of milk. She'd timed it perfectly. I had half a cookie and no milk left.

"Oh," she groaned, "that was wonderful. I feel sick."

We lay there for a long time recovering. Eventually we did have a coffee to settle our stomachs.

"So, Red, what're you doing tomorrow?"

I looked at my sheet. "I'm going to the Rivoli and the Old Firehall."

"Right. I want a full report." I thought she was being awfully good to take such an interest in me. Especially after the Stagewise thing.

"What are you going to do?" I asked.

"I'm going to look into acting lessons."

I told her what my improv teacher had said. That the way to learn to act was to act, and the way to learn to draw was to draw. Which I thought was pretty neat since he was a teacher.

"I agree with him in theory," she said, "but I've got to start somewhere. I want more than extra work."

"Yeah."

"Anyway, I gotta go." She grabbed her leather bag. "Look, we're having a party at our house Friday. All our friends are coming. Nerds mixed with freaks. You want to come?"

I didn't really. I hated parties.

"Sure," I said, "but I'm working Friday."

"Come after," she said, heading out the door. "It won't get rolling till midnight. Besides." She turned around and gave me one of her looks. "It might be a good night to lose your virginity."

Gulp.

EIGHT

THEY weren't at all interested in me at the Old Firehall. They couldn't understand what I was doing there when they hadn't advertised. They took my resume, though, and said they'd keep it on file. Resume. What a laugh. I hadn't done anything except Theatresports and the one Yuk Yuks thing, and that turned out not to blow them away as I'd planned.

The Rivoli was even worse. I thought I'd check it out first before talking to anyone, so I took a booth and ordered a cappuccino. Silvy always drank cappuccino. Frothy coffee. Everyone was in black, but not black like me. Serious black. No stickman curtain shorts for this crowd. They all looked bored, too. I figured there'd be no point trying to make these people laugh. They probably just wanted beatnik poetry about death. DEATH/ IS SOMETHING I LIVE WITH/ I LIVE WITH DEATH/ I LIVE FOR DEATH/ I'D DIE FOR DEATH. Arghh!

I paid my bill and left without even leaving my resume. When I walked out onto Queen Street I almost got knocked over by a couple of street vendors. Very clever street vendors. They were walking along with a neon pink ladder on their shoulders, and hanging from the ladder were a whole bunch of shorts made from bizarre material. They were stopped by a couple of women who actually bought a pair each. I thought this was pretty neat. There were other people selling shorts and T-shirts, but because these two moved around, you noticed them. A lot of people sold sunglasses

51

on the street, too. I suppose this was a good idea, although they were selling them so cheaply you had to wonder if they were hot. I still had the sunglasses Skye bought me for twenty-four dollars at Jackson Square. I'd had them three summers now.

I bought a turquoise and silver pinkie ring from a street vendor. Ten bucks. You have to spend money to perk yourself up in Toronto. You don't have to perk yourself up in Humbletown because in Humbletown you never have that feeling that something should be happening.

By the time Friday rolled around I actually hadn't gotten any further in my job search. Silvy liked to call it a job search. She said it made it seem less romantic.

Silvy wasn't at the Spaghetti Factory on Friday. All through my shift I was having second thoughts about the party. The crowds at the Factory were huge, and I was run off my feet. It seemed half of the audience for the O'Keefe came in to have dinner before the show and the other half after. I'd never been to the O'Keefe Centre. Silvy said it was more disappointing than sex.

When I took off my apron I was dead tired. I really didn't want to go to this party, but I didn't want to let Silvy down. She was the one and only friend I had.

There was no point in ringing the door bell or knocking because the house was positively pulsating. You could see it when you walked up the street. I'm amazed it didn't leave its foundations and shuffle off down the road. I opened the door and stuck my head in. The bike had been moved at least, but that didn't make that much difference to the hall in terms of space. The TV set was on, but the sound was off. At least I think it was off. The music was so loud it was impossible to tell. I felt like bolting. There'd be no problem with that since no one had noticed me.

There were a lot of older people at this party. By older I mean early twenties. It was a real mix. One guy looked like a physicist, or my idea of a physicist, anyway. He had fuzzy-wild hair and little gold-rimmed glasses. All he needed was a tweed jacket instead of the red T-shirt. One bony hand clutched a drink and the other bony hand held a cigarette. He *was* a physicist. When he turned around to talk to someone, I read his T-shirt. It had a couple of Bohr model drawings and underneath it said "stimulated emissions." It took me awhile.

I was starting to feel sick. Parties always made me nervous, but at least at the gang's old parties I could poke fun at the videos and make everyone laugh and get a hold of the situation. Sort of control it. This was like being a toothpick boat after a heavy rain. I might get swept into the living room with the smokers or flushed into the kitchen with the drinkers.

A favourite trick of mine came back to me. Go to the bathroom and think.

I made my way up the narrow staircase. When I accidently bumped into a guy and said "sorry," he of course said "anytime." Predictable. Luckily a girl with a buzz cut was just coming out of the bathroom, so I got in there and locked the door. It smelled weird. Smoke and booze, but something else, too. I pulled back the shower curtain and there in the tub was the source of the stink. Someone had puked in the bathtub. Little bits of orange like carrot cubes floating in yellow and brown. I started to gag. I fumbled with the door and burst out of there. When I feel sick like that I have to think of something else — roses in a vase, a beach with white sand and a blue sky — or else my mind drifts back to the puke and I can smell it again and I start to wretch.

Roses, roses, roses, I was thinking to myself when I spotted Silvy.

"Hey, Humbletown, you came!"

Of course I came. The thought that she didn't expect me to made me angry for a moment. To think I could've been back in my little room with only the heat and faint smell of garbage to deal with. She gave me a hug, though, so I forgave her instantly. I'm a sucker for body contact, though I don't like to initiate it myself. Probably because I'm so tall. If you're small you can snuggle into people, but if you're tall your arms kind of go around their shoulders and you end up hugging people's faces.

"Are you having a good time?" Silvy asked.

"Not really." She laughed.

"You need a drink."

"Not really."

I needed a couple of aspirin and a warm bath. The thought of a bath brought back the image of the puke in the tub and a wave of nausea swept over me. Roses, roses, roses. I followed Silvy down to the kitchen, which was packed, and she found a plastic glass and poured some horrible mixture into it from a milk jug. I sipped it. It burned but it was also sweet.

"What is this?" I shouted.

"Black Russians," she shouted back.

Suddenly the music switched from pulsating rock to just straight pulsating pulses. It was like a heartbeat blasting out from the two big speakers. Silvy rolled her eyes.

"Lucy and the anthropologists have taken over. This could go on for hours." I preferred it. Although I'd have given my eye teeth for Gene Kelly singin' in the rain.

I was wondering what would be a decent amount of time to stay without insulting my hostess. Half an hour? An hour? But I should have realized Silvy wouldn't have cared if I'd just stopped in to say hi and then left. There were clearly tons of parties in this house and clearly people turned up who didn't know anyone who even lived there. None of the etiquette my mother had tried to pass on to me was of any use here. Which is why, when Silvy somehow disappeared without having introduced me to anyone, I forgave her for that, too. I was standing in the kitchen intensely interested in the magnetic bugs on the side of the fridge when I heard a voice.

"You Lucy?" The voice went with a heavy-lidded face of a guy with a moustache.

"No. Sorry."

"Hey, that's okay." He wasn't going away. "You China?"

I shook my head. To save him from going through the list of people I might be, I said, "I don't live here." I looked around but I couldn't see Silvy. Heavy lids looked at my hair.

"Nice hair."

Botticelli hair, I thought. That's what Skye's stepfather Paul had called it the first time we met.

Way before I even knew who he was. He'd touched my hair and said, "Botticelli hair."

"Thanks," I said, and I brushed a hand through it. I wanted to leave but I felt safe in the bright light of the kitchen. Safe from what?

"How's your drink?"

"Fine," I said, sipping it. I felt stupid. Say nice hair and I touch my hair. Say how's the drink and I take a sip. I felt about thirteen years old.

"What's your name?"

"Kim."

"Short for Kimberly?" I nodded. "Hi, Kimberly. Jeremy." He held out his hand. I shook it, of course. Touch the hair, sip the drink, shake the hand. He didn't look like a Jeremy. When his parents named him they probably never figured on the moustache. His hand was cold.

"What year are you in, Kimberly?"

That was probably a technique. Repeat the name, so you remember it. So he assumed I was a student. This was disturbing. Did I look studious? I wanted to look like an up-and-coming actress, not a student. I'd have to wear more makeup. What was I going to say to this guy? I didn't want to tell the truth because certain people made me feel protective about my plans and he was one of those people. I didn't want to pretend I was in first year at university because it might get me into a lie I couldn't maintain. Maybe I could say grade nine, frighten him to death, and he'd leave me alone.

"1939," I said. He laughed. His teeth were very straight. I liked the laugh.

"Why 1939?"

"It was a great year for movies." This was a

mistake. Stringing words together to make a sentence is a definite signal of interest. I should've remembered that from high school. There's safety in monosyllables.

Once I'd opened myself up to him in this way, he wouldn't shut up. He talked on and on. About himself. He was a TA, Teaching Assistant in political science. It became clear to me that political science was just a study of politics, so why not call it political studies? At one point during a monologue on perestroika, he poured me another glassful from the milk jug. I avoided the obvious jokes about Black Russians, not wanting him to think I was head over heels in love.

Halfway through the second drink I started to actually feel pleased with myself. Here I was standing in a kitchen in Toronto, listening to jungle drum music and talking to a man about politics. He was a man, not a boy. He had a moustache and boozy breath and he talked about things of great importance. He said "consequently" a lot and "marginally." I felt grown up. I began to think I could even bring myself to do the things they did in the movies like put my hand on his cheek and give him a knowing smile, or toss my hair and laugh at something he said. He wasn't saying anything funny though. I had an overwhelming urge to lean on his shoulder, but instead I leaned against the fridge. It felt cool against my forehead.

My forehead. How did my forehead get on the fridge? Was I being rude? You should look at people when they talk to you even if it is about politics. I couldn't seem to get unstuck from the fridge. I tried to pull away but it was like my head was a big bug magnet.

I think I remember hands going around my waist. Man's hands. Jeremy's hands.

NINE

THE pounding in my head was not Lucy's anthro music. It was my own blood. Boomba, boomba, boomba. I was in bed, but not my own bed. This bed had greying sheets that were all bunched up and wrinkled. Silvy's bed. I was lying on my stomach with my mouth open. When I closed it, it tasted awful. And my teeth were fuzzy. I ran my dry tongue over them and it was like each one had its own little sweater. I knew I would eventually have to sit up, but I didn't want to yet.

So this was what a hangover was like. All those jokes my uncles made about it, all those songs like "Wasn't That a Party?" were wrong. There was nothing funny about this. I felt like I'd been beaten up, and I had no memory of getting into Silvy's bed. The no-memory part was almost worse than the pain, although that was bad. When I tried to lift my head, a pain shot up the side of my neck and into my right temple and throbbed there for awhile. I thought I might throw up, it hurt so much. Obviously I couldn't just lift my head. I'd have to wait for the throbbing to settle down, then turn myself over somehow. I felt like a turtle, only one with its shell on the front. I was stuck.

I think I went back to sleep again for awhile. When I woke up the second time things were marginally better. I'd lost my turtle-shell belly and was able to roll over onto my back. I didn't know what time it was. What day was it? Saturday. Friday night I'd worked till midnight, then gone to the party after, so this was Saturday. My first Saturday off in weeks and I had to spend it feeling rotten. What a colossal bummer.

I tried to sit up. It was agony, but I made it. I sat there on the edge of the bed for about ten minutes before I could move any further. My head felt heavy and painful. Not the darting, shooting stabs of pain when I first woke up — just one big ache. Like my head was a giant pumpkin. I tried to roll my pumpkin to the side, but that brought the nausea back so I had to just hold it very straight.

I managed to stand up. The room moved a little, then settled back down. I just didn't want to throw up. I hate throwing up. I inched my way to the door, which was open, and thought I heard some stirring downstairs. At the top of the stairs I grabbed onto the railing. I slowly, slowly made my way down, hanging onto the bannister with my right hand and gently running my left hand over the back of my neck. If I hit the right spot back there it sent a shiver all through me, ending in a cold sweat. The shiver and sweat was preferable to the solid heavy ache because it meant I could do something about my agony. Vary it a little.

At the bottom of the stairs I could hear whoever was in the kitchen moving back and forth. I got to the hallway entrance and there was the fridge. The site of my downfall. It was Silvy in the kitchen, drying a pile of plates. I hadn't heard her washing them, thank God. Clanking dishes was all I needed. She hadn't heard me because I'd moved so slowly.

"Hi, Silvy," I said. My voice came out crackly.

"Hey, Red," she said, turning quickly. "You look awful."

"I feel worse," I whispered. Silvy pushed a chair

against the counter for me and got a jug of orange juice out of the fridge. She poured a huge glass and put it in front of me.

"Drink," she said.

"I can't."

"Just sip. It'll make you feel better."

I'd have sipped carbolic acid if I'd thought it would make me feel better. I put my elbow on the counter and propped my head up and sipped the juice. Silvy must have known that just stacking the plates was too much for me because she stopped and let the rest air-dry. She made us a coffee and I sat there alternately sipping coffee and juice.

"When will I feel better?"

"You'll feel better by tonight, but you won't feel good till tomorrow night."

Great. I'd feel good again in time to scrape cold gluey pasta off dishes. *Roses, roses, roses.* It took me awhile to realize that Silvy had no makeup on. I'd never seen her without makeup. It was like she had no eyelashes. With a clean-scrubbed face and pink hair, she looked like a kid's doll. And she just had on jeans and a T-shirt. One of the ones she'd painted herself. No leather. She looked cute, a word I'd never have used about her before. Her comps should have shown her like this.

The makeuplessness made me realize my face was probably a fright. I licked the end of my shirt and ran it under my eyes. The advantage of wearing black.

"What are you doing?" Silvy asked.

"Getting rid of my raccoon eyes," I said.

"I took care of that last night." I just looked at her. "I would never let you go to bed with makeup on, Kim. It's bad for you." I couldn't help laughing

61

even though it hurt my head. She'd taken care of my black mascara but hadn't worried about Black Russians.

"Well, I didn't know you were going to suck them back like sody-pop!" She'd reminded me. How did I get upstairs? How did Silvy get my makeup off? I had no memory of it.

"The guy with the moustache carried you upstairs and I did you with cold cream and a face cloth."

"What kind of person takes a drunk's makeup off?"

"A very considerate person."

"That's hilarious. I wish I'd been there. What did Jeremy think?"

"That's his name? He thought you were a visionary who understood that the world is on the brink of catastrophe."

Oh, God. The 1939 comment. He was thinking World War Two and I was thinking Gone With the Wind. I had to go to the bathroom. I'd managed two orange juices and a cup of coffee. I didn't want to go upstairs, though. It would make me sick.

"I cleaned the tub out," Silvy said, reading my mind. Silvy hadn't had any sleep at all. The last guest had left around eight in the morning. No, that wasn't entirely true. When I stood up to try to make it to the bathroom, I saw a couple of bodies in the living room.

"Who they?"

"I don't know. They came in after you conked out. They haven't woken up yet."

"What time is it?"

"After two."

"Two?" I couldn't believe it. Two? I must have slept twelve hours.

Silvy had done a fine job on the bathroom. It smelled of cleanser. When I washed my hands I caught sight of myself in the mirror. I didn't have raccoon eyes, true, but I had almost no eyes at all. Gone With the Bloat. I needed cucumber slices but I knew Silvy wouldn't have any.

When I got back downstairs she'd poured me another orange juice.

"You've got to keep the liquids going. You're dehydrated." I took it and opened her fridge. No cukes. I grabbed some soy sauce packets and took them into the living room and stretched out on the couch that had no bodies on it. I put a packet on each eye and two on my forehead. Very soothing.

When I woke up for the third time that day it was to the sound of bodies stirring. They were girls. No one had removed their makeup for them. They stretched and ran their hands through their hair, scratching. I recognized them.

"Hey," I said. "I know you! You're the shorts people!" They were the ones I'd seen walking around with shorts hanging from a ladder on their shoulders. Silvy came in just then with a couple of shopping bags.

"Who's for toast and coffee?" she said. I figured a little toast would slide down all right. I had to get something in my poor stomach.

"Silvy, these girls sell shorts on the street."

"Hi," she said.

"Hi," they said. "Is this your house?"

"I share it."

"Thanks for the party."

"You're welcome."

They were going to leave, but I couldn't let them. I wanted to talk to them. They were the first street vendors I'd met personally. Silvy couldn't understand what the excitement was about, but when I asked them to stay for coffee she didn't give me a scathing look or anything. She just made coffee for everyone while I quizzed the shorts people about how they got going, how they got a licence, how much money they made. They made lots of money because the shorts were so easy to make. Two pieces sewn together and an elastic waist. A piece of cake. Like my stickman shorts.

"Silvy, Silvy, don't you see? You sell your T-shirts this way!"

"Kim, you think I haven't thought of that? There's a million hand-painted T-shirts out there. Why would anyone buy mine?"

"You need a gimmick," one of the girls said.

"Yeah," the other said. "We hardly broke even till we thought up the ladder thing."

"Well, there's nothing new to do with T-shirts," Silvy said.

"Silvy!" I tried to swallow my dry wad of toast. I wasn't feeling good at all, but my excitement was overriding my misery. "You've got the greatest gimmick in the world!"

"What?"

"Me!"

TEN

ONCE I've made a decision, I like to act on it. I thought we should quit our jobs and hit the streets. Silvy was full of doubts. We shouldn't cut ourselves off from the Spaghetti Factory, just in case. What would we do in a couple of months when it got cold?

All of these were of no interest to me. I figured we'd sign up with Kelly Girl, which would be better anyway.

"No one wants a pink-haired receptionist. Besides, you need a working wardrobe. You can't work in an office in cutoffs and T-shirts. And anyway, I can't stand offices."

I finally got a hundred dollars out of her and I put in a hundred dollars and we bought some white cotton T-shirts, all large, and paint. We decided our first run would be Marilyn Monroe. Silvy could get Marilyn in a few lines. She did the famous winking one from "Gentlemen Prefer Blondes." She was really good. We splurged on a little yellow and silver paint. A line of yellow for hair and some silver on the eyelids.

I left Silvy in my room painting while I went searching for a blond wig. The kind of wigs you find at Amity and Salvation Army are only good for Halloween. I did find a pair of long white evening gloves, though, which I snapped up for seventy-nine cents. In despair I went to Eaton's. There was the perfect wig there. Two hundred and thirty-nine dollars. Arghh. I tried it on.

"Hi. I'm Marilyn. Pleased to meet you, I'm sure."

"May I help you?"

A woman with her mouth all pinched appeared behind the counter.

"Will you take a cheque?"

"Do you have an Eaton's card?"

"No."

"Visa?"

"No."

"Mastercard?"

"Sorry." This could go on all day.

"Then I'm afraid you'll have to pay cash." She held out her hands, but I didn't want to take off the wig.

"Does that come with it?" I pointed to the bald Styrofoam face.

"Well . . ."

"I'll go get cash from the machine," I said.

"All right."

I took off my wig and gave it to her. She put it back on the Styrofoam face.

"But I'll only hold it for fifteen minutes," she said, putting it under the counter. Part of me didn't really think the throngs would be fighting for a platinum blond wig, but part of me wanted it so badly I thought someone else might, too.

"I'll be right back."

I tore out to the nearest machine. CIBC. I'd have to use Interac and be charged another dollar. I was just about to punch in two-forty when I remembered tax. Oh, God. I punched in two-sixty. This was ridiculous. Silvy would have a fit. I looked at my little withdrawal slip. I had $519.23 left. Take the rent off that in two weeks and I'd barely have two hundred bucks. But I still had a cheque to come for one-eighty from Spaghetti Factory, and if I didn't quit till after this week, another one-eighty after that. Anyway, it was done now. The money was out of my account and if I didn't buy the wig I'd just spend it on something stupid like food.

I ran back to the counter and the same woman was there. She handed me my wig and Styrofoam face and I handed her, gulp, $258.12.

When I got back to my room, Silvy'd done a couple of shirts. They looked great. She was so pleased with them she'd signed them in the lower left corner. Silvy X, just like on my wall.

"What'd you buy at Eaton's?" she said, noticing my bag.

"The perfect wig."

"New?"

"Yeah."

"You bought it new? That must've cost a fortune."

"Yeah."

"Kim."

"Wait'll you see it!" I tore out into the bathroom. In the ghastly pink it didn't look quite as amazing, but I wasn't upset. I was getting used to that mirror. It made a blackhead look like the Sea of Tranquility. Silvy was in agreement about the beauty of the wig, but ticked off about the cost.

"You have to spend money to make money. Look what the shorts girls did with that ladder."

"Kim, the ladder cost them ten bucks and the Day-Glo spray paint about five. They paid for their ladder with two sales. We'd have to sell fifty

T-shirts to break even and we only *bought* fifteen!" We'd decided on a five-dollar profit per shirt.

"I'm paying for the wig out of my own money."

"No, you're not. We're in this together. Only from now on we clear all purchases with each other, okay?"

"Over ten dollars." I had my eye on the perfect lipstick.

"Over ten dollars."

Silvy got back to work. It was fun to see the shirts piling up. Our inventory. I could just see the headlines. *Fashion maven Silvy X credits Oscar nominee Kimberly Taylor with her success.* Silvy would design and custom fit all my clothes for me. I'd be sewn into my Oscar night gown, of mint-green silk to offset my flaming tresses, by Silvy herself. Once I won the Oscar, I'd insist that she do the wardrobe for all my films.

Wardrobe. I had to put together the rest of Marilyn's costume for, I had to face it, nothing. At least I already had the gloves. I hadn't seen anything in the way of dresses at the Goodwill or Sally Ann, either. I thought it was going to be tough. Then I remembered my sister was at that age where all her friends were dropping like flies. She must've been a bridesmaid three times in the last year.

"Never a blushing bride," Kathy sang when I phoned her up. "How you doing, kid?"

"Great."

"Got any starring parts?"

"Oh, yeah, I did a very important scene in a movie a couple of weeks ago."

"Really?"

"Yeah. Me and sixty others."

68

"It's a start."

I told Kathy what I wanted and offered to pay.

"Listen, kid, you can have all of them."

"Really?"

"Sure. Why don't you come to Mum's for dinner tomorrow?"

I could do it. My shift was eleven to five and the express bus would have me there by six-thirty, but I didn't really want to spend the money. Kathy guessed why I was hesitating.

"You buy your ticket home and I'll put you back on at this end," she said. It was a deal. Neither of us had mentioned Skye.

"You want to come?" I asked Silvy, but she was working. I wasn't sure what my dad would make of her hair, anyway. My mum wouldn't mind as long as it was clean.

"Aren't you nervous, Humbletown?" she said. I just looked at her. "You'll get back to your cosy old house. Your mum will have made your favourite meal. Your brother will be nice to you. It's not even the end of August. School won't start for another couple of weeks. You could slip back in without anyone knowing you'd even left."

This was unkind. All this because I'd confessed that whenever the Back-to-School signs appeared in stores, I was overcome with the three-ring binder urge. And hilighters. I loved hilighting.

"I'm strong," I said. "Besides, I'm doing this for the company." That's how we referred to ourselves. The Company.

"Well, we'll see, won't we?" Silvy said. Then she got back to painting shirts.

ELEVEN

STEPPING off the bus at Grandad's Donuts was weird, but walking down Dundurn was weirder. I'd only been gone a little over a month, but it felt a lot longer. My buddies in front of the liquor store had called it a day, which was too bad. I wanted to tell them I'd be joining them soon. Taking money from people passing by. Could I really do it? I got a little shiver just thinking about it. Of course, I wouldn't just be taking, as Silvy pointed out. They'd be getting fine-quality T-shirts and a side show to boot. I was the side show.

"Kim!" My mum gave me a great big hug. Then my dad, then Kathy. Even Jamie hugged me. He must've been coached. It was very strange to have their focussed attention. Usually they went about their day unless you said something wildly funny or threw up, but I'd just walked in the house for Pete's sake.

"How's the room?"

"Looks great."

"How's the Spaghetti Factory?"

"Fine, fine."

"Have you made any friends?"

"There's this neat girl, Silvy — "

"Why don't you have her home for dinner?" *I already did. My home.*

"She's working tonight. At the Spaghetti Factory. She's an actress, too." *Too. That's rich.*

Silvy was absolutely right about dinner. My mum made my favourite. Barbecued chicken and blueberry pie. At least it had been my favourite when

70

I was a kid. I was developing quite a taste for eggplant. I made them laugh with a few Spaghetti Factory stories, but I skipped the party. I also decided not to mention the street theatre. I liked the sound of that. Street Theatre. It sounded so much more dignified than pedling.

After dinner Kathy and I went up to our old room to try on the dresses. It was weird being in that room with Kathy and being allowed on the side with the mirror. I tried on the turquoise number first. It was shiny clingy material with a slit right up the middle and sleeves like little capes off each shoulder.

"Isn't that incredible?" Kathy said. She was sprawled across the bed. "Carmen said she chose that so we could wear it again! Where would I wear that?"

There was a good line there, but I let it go because I was busy visualizing this dress without the dippy sleeves. Without the sleeves it would have a distinct fifties look. I'd need a lot of padding for Marilyn, but I expected that. The other two dresses were that particular shade of fuchsia favoured by bridal parties everywhere. And, again, the material was slinky and slithery. I took them all, because Kathy said I could, but the turquoise one had the most potential. She'd brought the shoes but they didn't fit because my feet were a size larger than hers.

"I miss this mirror," I said.

"I miss this room," Kathy said. I couldn't imagine why, since she'd never had it all to herself like I had.

"Really? Why don't you sleep here then?" I

resisted the urge to say she might as well since she ate here most nights.

"Don't laugh, it's tempting."

"How's work?" I decided to get the conversation off Life on Your Own, since I was having a whale of a time.

"Oh, okay."

"Still on orthopedics?"

"Yeah."

After Skye had tried to kill herself, she ended up on Kathy's ward, for privacy. If she hadn't, I'd never have found out about it. No one but a few nurses and doctors would have ever known. And then it wouldn't have been so unbearable for me at school and maybe I'd be heading back to grade twelve this fall.

Nah. This had always been my plan. Skye and her wicked stepfather only speeded things up.

"What are you thinking about?" Kathy asked.

"Skye."

"I guess you never heard from her."

"My letters came back unopened. I bet she never saw them."

"Those assholes."

It was weird being in our old room talking. Kathy had always seemed so big and grownup to me. We never talked in that room. I stayed on my side and watched her put on her makeup, but we never talked.

She said she'd drive me to the bus. When I got downstairs everyone was lined up to say goodbye. My mum had a box with the rest of the pie in it. My dad said, "Your room's always here, doll," and gave me a hug and twenty dollars. Even Jamie was standing there looking dorky, so I gave him a hug,

72

too. I was glad to get in the car with Kathy. I opened the pie box and there was a twenty-dollar bill with a Post-it note saying I LOVE YOU on it from my mum.

"Whew," I said to Kathy, "that was quite a scene. I'm amazed Ron wasn't there to complete the picture."

"Ron's got a lot on his mind these days."

"Oh, yeah?"

"Yeah. Debbie's pregnant."

"Pregnant?" Debbie was Ron's girlfriend. She was just a little older then me. And pregnant. They hadn't planned to get married for a few years. Until she finished high school.

"Are they going to get married?"

"Probably. Soon."

"Gee. Maybe I should save the fuchsia numbers and you and I can be bridesmaids." Kathy gave me a look. I couldn't help myself.

"Well, well, well. Ronny will be a father. We'll be aunts!"

"Old maid aunts."

"Yuck.'"

"Double yuck."

"You're not exactly an old maid, Kathy."

"No."

"How old were you when you lost it?"

"What? Ki-im!"

"C'mon, we're having a heart to heart here. We're going to be aunties. How old were you?"

"Fifteen."

"*What*?" I was truly boggled. "You mean, while we were sharing a room, you were . . ."

"Yeah."

"Did Mum know?"

"Are you kidding? She'd have died. Don't you tell her."

"No, no. I won't tell." I sat there in shock. At the same age I'd got myself a serious girlfriend, Kathy'd got herself a serious boyfriend. No wonder Silvy was amazed by me. Even my own sister hadn't been a GLV. And now my brother was pregnant. Where was I while all this was going on? I felt like I'd just found out I'd been living in a different dimension.

"You're still a virgin, aren't you?" Kathy asked. Why pretend?

"Yeah."

"I thought so."

"How come?"

"You're having so much fun. You haven't had a big disappointment yet." I didn't tell her about Brad. She was sounding just like Silvy.

"Is it so disappointing?"

"Eventually. Fifteen was great. Twenty was the pits."

I didn't like this kind of talk. I liked to think life just got better and better. So far, for me, it had.

We parked across from the bus station. Kathy came in with me and bought my ticket. I was happy she'd remembered, but I wasn't going to remind her. She walked with me to the bus. Bay three, express to Toronto. It was already in. I was a little overloaded with my pie and dresses, but Kathy was reaching into her purse. She pulled out a twenty.

"Oh, no, Kathy, I couldn't."

"C'mon."

"Mum and Dad gave me some. I'm okay."

"So? Let me do this. I make lots of money. Take

74

advantage of it before I get married and have ten kids."

"When you put it that way . . ."

I turned sideways and she stuffed the twenty in my pants pocket. Everyone was sure being nice. Kathy gave me a hug around my packages and I gave the driver my ticket and climbed on. When the bus pulled out and rounded the corner, I saw her leaving the parking lot.

It's amazing how you can live in the same house with someone and not know what's going on with them. Was Kathy happy? Was Ron happy? I'd never even thought about it before.

At Dundurn and King there was an elaborate billboard. It said, "People from Toronto think: that Hamilton is a city of streets all going the wrong way; that the Jolley Cut is a new way to slice roast beef; that nothing ever happens until *they* move here." It was put up by the Hamilton *Spectator*. Wow. Never mind *Hamilton, the ambitious city*. Now it was *Hamilton, the angry city*.

By the time the bus was on the QEW I wasn't thinking about my family or Humbletown anymore. I was thinking about my routine. With padding and the gloves and a mole on my cheek, I'd be ready to do Marilyn. I started to hum to myself. Diamonds Are a Girl's Best Friend.

TWELVE

"YOU look fabulous!" Silvy was circling me with her mouth open. "Say something for me."

"Something for me."

"C'mon."

I sang. "I'M JUST A LI'L GAL FROM L'IL ROCK. HI. I JUST LOVE PINK HAIR. IT TURNS MY LIMBS TO JELLY."

"I always thought you leaned a little that way, Mare."

"OH! WHY, YOU CRAZY GIRL! PLEASED TO MAKE YOUR ACQUAINTANCE, I'M SURE."

"Kim, you've got her. You've really got her."

"Yeah. I just wish I had her nose."

"No, no. When I look at you I *see* Marilyn Monroe."

"THAT'S THE IDEA, HONEY. Besides, the nose comes in handy for Cher. You like the wig?"

"Worth every penny."

Silvy was great. She even showed me how to put contour powder down the middle of my nose to minimize it. Dark makes things fade, light brings things out, she said. My makeup was really light, so it's good I have fair skin. We covered the freckles with my own foundation, then put a lighter one on top and lots of powder. We did the mole with eyebrow pencil. I'd dyed the evening gloves turquoise and had to settle on strappy gold high heels from Amity for shoes. The padding on the chest was fun, but the padding on the bum was hilarious. I couldn't keep my hands off my newly acquired hips. With the little capes gone from the shoulders, the dress even looked like something Marilyn might have worn.

Silvy didn't want to work out a routine. She figured the faster we hit the streets the better. The first day we had off together was Sunday. Where would we go?

"Harbourfront!" said Silvy, and it was decided.

Saturday night I hardly slept even though I'd worked till midnight again. But I was too excited. And when I did nod off I dreamed I was doing Marilyn.

What I hadn't prepared for was taking the subway dressed like a tart at nine in the morning. With me in my platinum hair and Silvy in her pink hair, we attracted more attention than we wanted. At least I'd had the brains to throw a raincoat on and cover up that sleazy dress, but it made me hot, so by the time we got to Harbourfront I was fairly cranky.

"You try walking in these things," I said to Silvy, who was in sneakers and cutoffs and a T-shirt. She was also lugging most of our stuff.

"Hey, girls, can I take you home?" Arghh! This was not what I had intended. Silvy rolled off a few expletives at the jerk who'd said it.

We finally got set up right across from the antique market. Silvy had a folding chair and a little makeup box for money. We set up under a bunch of trees for shade and pegged a couple of shirts on the branches. They really were beautiful. I knew Silvy had tried to sell her stuff before without a lot of success. I hoped this would work out.

"These are great!" a voice said. It was another

77

street vendor. She was selling sunglasses. "Who are you?" she said to me.

"HI. I'M MARILYN. PLEASED TO MEET YOU, I'M SURE." I held my hand out and she shook it and laughed, then looked at Silvy.

"Great gimmick," she said and wandered back to her spot. It's weird, but I didn't feel at all stuck or nervous like I had that time at Theatresports, and I think I know why. Because it wasn't me out there. It was Marilyn!

As it got on for ten o'clock the spaces filled up. One family had a great idea. They had a beautiful cart with all their homespun wool on it and the mother sat there and knitted and the daughter would spin and the father worked the crowd. Ali-Kat was the name on their cart. I figured the women's names were probably Alison and Kate or something like that.

Silvy and I had got a lot of looks but no one stopped until I spotted a couple come out of the antique market and stop in their tracks. I gave them a little Marilyn wave and they looked at each other and came over. The woman just kept laughing and laughing. I flirted with the man and called him Sugar and his wife took a picture of us together. I tilted my head back and put my arms around his funny little head. He was shorter than me. They were having a hoot.

"You must be American," they kept saying.

"I'M JUST A L'IL GAL FROM L'IL ROCK."

"Can we take you home?"

"YOU *CAN* TAKE ME HOME, SUGAR, IN THE FORM OF THIS BEAUTIFUL T-SHIRT." Inspired. I held it to my chest. "IT'LL BE LIKE HAVING YOUR VERY OWN MARILYN RIGHT NEXT TO YOUR

HEART. BOOPA DEE BOO, BOOPA DEE BOO." He handed over fifteen dollars without blinking. Then his wife said, "Get one for Maisie, she'd love it," and he peeled off another fifteen. When they got in their car I blew them a little kiss.

"They took my picture!" I said to Silvy.

"They bought two shirts!" she said. We grabbed each other by the arms. I thought I was going to burst. This was fun. And it was so easy!

While Silvy was off getting us some coffee, I noticed that the girl to the left of us hadn't sold any of her sponge dogs yet. She was making one of them sit up and beg when she packed up all of a sudden and left. I didn't know why until I looked down the line and saw two police officers walking along and stopping now and then.

They were checking for licences. We didn't have one! I closed my eyes and wished Silvy would hurry. There was no way I could pack our things up on my own and disappear. The hot dog vendors were okay. Their licences were displayed on their carts. The guy selling jewellery reached into his cash box and pulled out something. The cops nodded and handed it back. Then they were standing in front of me. Gulp.

"OH, GOLLY. A POLICEMAN." They looked at each other. "EVER SO PLEASED TO MAKE YOUR ACQUAINTANCE, I'M SURE." This was called stalling. "EVERYONE! LET'S GIVE A BIG HAND TO OUR BOYS IN BLUE." I was clapping like crazy but no one else was. "I JUST LOVE A MAN IN UNIFORM." Oh, God. If my mother could see me she'd die.

"Can we see your licence, Marilyn?" one cop said. That was nice. The other one wasn't even smiling. They were playing Good Cop, Bad Cop.

"LICENCE? BUT I DON'T DRIVE, OFFICER. I'M JUST A L'IL GAL FROM L'IL ROCK."

Silvy turned up with a coffee in each hand.

"OH, GOSH, SILVY, I THINK THESE TWO NICE GENTLEMEN ARE GOING TO GIVE ME A PARKING TICKET!"

"Not if you have a licence."

"We have a licence." Silvy put down the coffees and reached into her bag. One of them checked it out while I held my breath. He nodded.

"See how easy life is when you go by the book?" he said.

"GOLLY, YES, I ALWAYS GO BY THE BOOK. THANKS EVER SO."

The Good Cop smiled and they moved on.

"Where did you get the licence?" I whispered at Silvy.

"I told you I tried to sell my T-shirts before. This spring." She handed me a coffee. It tasted so good. My feet hurt a little. They were toughened up from the Spaghetti Factory but they weren't used to high heels on pavement. I looked at the licence. Pedlar's Licence it actually said.

"We're pedlars!"

"Yep."

"Can we put that on our income tax? Pedlar?"

"Why not? They'll like it better than 'actress,' believe me."

I was having such a wonderful time. I was pedling in the sun with my friend Silvy and pretending to be Marilyn Monroe and, sort of, getting paid for it. Surely an agent would go by and see me. She'd hand me her card and when I went to her office next day she wouldn't recognize me.

"I'm Marilyn," I'd say, and she'd gasp.

"My God," she'd say, "you're Marilyn? I was thinking of you for a commercial — doing your Marilyn impersonation — but now that I see you face to face, I have just the part for you!"

I'd sign on with her and do the movie. It wouldn't be a box office success, but I would be noticed. Every reviewer would say, "In the small but significant role of Emily, Kimberly Taylor shines. We look forward to seeing more of her." Then the offers would start to pour in. I'd have to pick and choose carefully, selecting only those parts which would help me stretch and grow as an actress.

THIRTEEN

HAVING to work six to midnight after a full day on the street was awful. In one of our famous intermittent conversations I tried to convince Silvy to quit the Spaghetti Factory.

"We can't do both. It's too grueling . . ."

"It's not for me, I just sit there and watch you . . ."

"...Silvy! You make our T-shirts! When are you going to get more done . . ."

"...we only sold four today, Kim. There's not a big demand . . ."

Oh, dear. It was true that I got a lot of attention and by and large most people hadn't bought T-shirts.

"...this was our first day! Wait till we get a reputation . . ."

"...what are we going to do when winter comes . . ."

"...we'll sell sweatshirts. They'll love it . . ."

"...are you going to do Marilyn in an overcoat . . ."

"...not Marilyn. We'll do White Christmas . . ."

"...no one wants a sweatshirt with Bing Crosby on it, Red."

She had a point there. But I'd had such a great time. I had to face it, I was hooked. I also had to face the fact that while Silvy had gone along with me and been great about everything, she probably wasn't going to stick with it. This proved to be true a couple of weeks later. We had actually sold all fifteen of our T-shirts. That meant we'd made seventy-five dollars which still left the company three hundred and eighty dollars in the hole. Plus we had to buy more shirts for the second run. Economically it wasn't making a lot of sense.

The second run was Sonny and Cher, which didn't require any money for my part, just labour. I worked hard on that costume. Basically one pair of jeans did for both of them, but I painted flowers on Cher's side and ripped it at the knee. Silvy donated a fake fur vest that was just perfect. Underneath it I wore an old T-shirt cut in half up to above the belly button on the Cher side, and stitched so it wouldn't unravel. The hair was easy because of an old witch's wig that Kathy and I had both used on Halloween that had sat in the basement for years. Sonny wore a ripped sneaker and Cher went barefoot. Red toe nails, of course.

Silvy's shirts were fabulous. Again, she managed to get Cher in a couple of lines and Sonny was this tiny little figure looking up at her. I always really raved about them and she knew they were great, but the fact is people were stopping because of me.

We were on the corner of Yonge and St. Clair. All the boomers were buzzing around in their suits even though it was another blazing hot day, and I started singing "I Got You Babe." I'd turn one way to show the Cher half and sing with that low tremor she does. Then I'd turn to show the Sonny half and sing in his little squeak.

They went nuts. There must've been a three-deep lineup around our corner. Mostly guys in suits, but the odd woman in a suit, too. I switched to "The Beat Goes On," and when I got to the lahdeedahdeedahs, they went nuts again. Everyone joined in. There we were, about thirty of us on the corner of Yonge and St. Clair, singing Lahdeedah-deedah Lahdeedahdeedee. It was like a powerful drug. I wanted more.

And then the amazing thing happened. Some of them started reaching into their pockets. Two-dollar bills, even the odd ten, were slapped into my hands. I could hardly believe it. By the time the last person had drifted away saying, "See you, Son," or "Bye, Cher," I thought I'd wet myself with excitement. I turned to Silvy with my mittful of money.

Oh, God. Not one person had bought a T-shirt. Not one.

I started folding out the money and putting it in the makeup box. Fifty-five dollars. Wow. We'd have to sell eleven T-shirts to clear that much. I didn't know what to say.

"You were great, Kim."

"Thanks," I said, and then I looked at her. She had little tears in her eyes. Tough, pink-haired Silvy with the eye makeup was on the verge of crying.

"Silvy . . ."

I was going to say I was sorry I hadn't sold any shirts, that I'd got carried away, but she just said, "It's okay," and disappeared into the mall, leaving me with the money and the shirts and the chair and the TV table we'd picked up.

I knew how she felt. I knew how I'd felt when Skye wowed everyone in improv class and wiped me off the map. And her shirts were so good.

But people didn't want really good shirts. What did people want?

"'I Got You Babe.'"

I turned around. There were five people standing there. Three men and two women. I did it for them. What's amazing is, I did it as well as I'd done it the first time even though my mind was really on Silvy. That was weird. To be able to switch on like that. But I guess it's no different than going to school knowing you're the class dork and cracking jokes anyway. Besides, I was getting paid for it.

"Sorry I just took off like that," Silvy said that night at the Spaghetti Factory. We were taking our break in the parking lot. They didn't like us doing it, but you had to get out sometimes.

"That's okay," I said. "I sold four shirts."

"Really?"

"Yeah."

This wasn't entirely true. I'd sold two and bought two myself. One for Mum and one for Kathy.

"How did you get home?"

"I managed." There was a significant pause.

"Kim, I really think you should go on your own."

"No."

"Listen to me. I want to save up my money and take acting lessons. I *don't* want to sell crummy T-shirts — "

"They're not crummy. That's why you're upset."

"Yeah. Well. My point is, you've got something people want. And that's great. How's the job search going?"

"Oh, I dropped that ages ago." I told her about it.

"Maybe you should stick to the streets. Maybe a club will come to you instead of you going to it."

"Do you really think so?"

"Sure. Why not? You've got talent, Red." Talent. Silvy was the first person to say that to me. Lots of people said it later, but Silvy said it first.

FOURTEEN

So I took to the streets. When a pink-haired oracle speaks, I listen. Besides, I loved it.

It came to me why I was good at it. It was like that time at Theatresports when my partner Jane got sick and I made up a whole team myself. There was no one else jumping in with an idea that would screw up my plans. I was better on my own.

I quit the Spaghetti Factory. Being a decent girl from Humbletown, I gave them two weeks' notice instead of hanging up my apron like my predecessor. Silvy thought I was nuts, but I figured this way, when I was famous, the roving tabloid reporters wouldn't be able to snoop around in my past and turn up a story: *Stuck-up Star Left Job in a Huff.* I actually thought about that kind of thing. Also, being at the Spaghetti Factory I could still see a lot of Silvy, if intermittently. I knew it wouldn't be quite the same once I'd left. She absolutely refused to take back the money she'd put in the company. "Consider it an early investment by your manager," she said.

Not all days were as good as that one at Yonge and St. Clair, but the memory of the good ones kept me going through the bad ones. Some areas, of course, were better than others. And some were magic. The Beaches was not magic. The Beaches is this part of town near, appropriately enough, a beach. But the people there either do not like street theatre or they're terminally shy. They seemed suspicious of me. I set up outside a little frozen yogurt place and they went by in droves

87

without stopping. They seemed to glance out at me from the corners of their eyes as though I was a bag lady. Someone who might pee on their nice sidewalks or something. I didn't go back.

As bad as the Beaches was, a certain area of Bloor Street was magic. I set up across the street from the Lick'n Chicken. This was my magic spot and it was very tempting to stay put, but I had this notion I should be seen everywhere. Most people gave money at this spot, though in smaller amounts. Fifty cents here and a dollar there, but that was great. I remembered the couple I'd given twenty-five cents to in Jackson Square back in Hamilton. I'd felt badly about it but I wouldn't now. Twenty-five cents is better than nothing. There was a time of night on that corner that was just wonderful. A lot of times people would want to stop and talk, which was fine by me because it meant a bit of a break.

That was how I met Jesus.

"You're very funny," a quiet young guy said. He had on a blue Hawaiian shirt and gold-rimmed glasses. He had a buzz cut.

"Thanks," I said. I wasn't scared of people on the street. I was scared in the subway and scared going back to my room, but when I was out there, one of them, I wasn't scared at all.

"You must see a lot of movies," he said. That was because one of my most popular routines was "YOUR FAVOURITE MOVIE IN FIVE MINUTES." There had to be some use for all those old movies I'd watched. Musicals were the most requested, which was good because it was easier to move from point to point in a story by just bursting into a few bars of song. Hardly anyone ever asked for a porn movie, but I came up with a way to handle them when they did. I made a black thing for my eyes and a "censored" sign. I'd hold them up, get a quick laugh, then point to someone else to name their favourite movie.

"Have you ever seen 'The Greatest Story Ever Told'?"

Oh, God, years ago. Maybe I could get him onto 'Ten Commandments' without him noticing. I do a mean Moses. These were the thoughts racing through my head when he dropped his little bombshell.

"It's about me."

I just looked at him. It still hadn't hit me. So he spelled it out.

"I'm Jesus."

"Oh." *Really?*

"Really."

"Oh." *This guy's a full tilt loony.*

"You don't believe me."

"Oh, I don't know." *Sure I do, just don't cut my face.*

"That's okay. Most people don't." He looked so sad. Incredibly sad. "When I first got the stigmata," he touched his palms, "I knew."

I nodded. I'd heard of that. I'd heard that people actually bled from the places where Jesus had been wounded. Maybe it had happened to this guy. That didn't mean he *was* Jesus. I didn't say so, though.

"I put on a white robe and I walked up Bathurst. I got quite a gathering. People actually followed me. They knew."

Wow. This guy was intense. I was kind of hoping

89

someone would come by and ask for a routine and kind of interested in what happened next to Jesus.

"I went to someone I thought would understand. I went to my minister." This is where Jesus showed a lack of judgement.

"What happened?" I couldn't believe I asked that. That's definitely called *encouraging them*. But he looked so sad.

"He had me locked up."

"Prison?"

"The Clarke." Even a relative newcomer to Toronto like me knew what that meant. Crazy people.

"I'm sorry," I said. I was. I didn't like to think of this nice gentle-looking guy in a blue Hawaiian shirt locked up just for a little thing like believing he was Jesus. I mean, if he'd believed he was Hitler I'd have wrestled him to the ground myself.

"'Gone With the Wind,'" someone called out, and I thought I recognized the voice but I didn't have time to think about that. Like a reflex action I was into it. I'd done 'Gone With the Wind' a couple of times and it was pretty much automatic. What was really exciting was when someone called out one I hadn't done before.

Atlanta was burning before I realized Jesus had gone. He certainly wasn't pushy.

Some days I only made ten dollars, but most days I got over forty. I could hardly believe it. The strangest thing about working the streets is that the other street people don't bother you. They leave you alone. I watched once while a guy came along Bloor stopping everyone and asking for a quarter. I was standing there with my Movie in Five Minutes sign and a quarter ready to give him.

He walked right by! I wasn't a mark because I was on his side. I was amazed by that. Of course, when I wasn't set up for performing, and especially when I was out of my usual territory, I got hit up all the time. It got so I regularly got a roll of quarters at the bank and had them with me to put into the open hands. I've hardly ever given anyone a quarter that they didn't fall all over themselves to thank me and say "Bless you, dear." For a quarter, for God's sake. As if they could get anything with a quarter.

As it got colder I stayed mainly in the Bloor-Bathurst area. You get your favourite territory. One mean day in November, when no one was asking for any movies, a guy came out of Book City and gave me a coffee. There was a lot of that. I saw Jesus once more in November. He just started talking to me again as though we'd left off our conversation a moment ago.

"I got kicked out of my apartment," he said with that sad look.

"I'm sorry," I said.

"The landlord spat on me."

"Oh." I was going to say, "Oh, Jesus," but I stopped myself.

"Why would anyone spit on me?" He looked at me with those sad bewildered eyes. He really had no idea. Part of me wanted to joke and say, "It's just like the first time, isn't it?" and part of me was a little scared that he might freak out. But a bigger part of me thought he was just a nice guy who thought he was Jesus. So what? I got so carried away sometimes I almost thought I was Scarlett O'Hara. But I was never that convincing. Maybe he *was* Jesus. Anyway, he disappeared again for a long time. I hoped he wasn't back at the Clarke.

One woman started coming by once a week asking for "White Christmas." She always put five dollars in the hat. Yes, I bought a special hat for this purpose. A top hat from the Sally Ann. In windy weather I weighted it down with a rock.

Another woman wanted Bogie and Bacall all the time. "Key Largo," "The Big Sleep," "To Have and Have Not" — whatever I felt like doing. She was such a regular that I put together a special costume. Half Bogie, half Bacall. I got an old suit, also from Sally Ann, and cut it in half. I sewed it to a blouse and half skirt and also got a slinky dressing gown just for the whistling scene in "To Have and Have Not." I slicked back half of my hair with goop and half I smoothed under and pinned like a pageboy. Half my face was made up and I put a little stubble on the other half with my kohl pencil. My lady nearly went wild when she saw me, and she left me a ten-dollar bill.

I was feeling terrific enough as it was, when one of her friends came back and asked what I charged for private parties. Without even thinking I named a price.

"Fifty dollars." He thought a bit.

"Twenty-five and we pass the hat."

"It's a deal."

It was a deal I never regretted. I made seventy-five dollars that night. And that night led to other nights.

FIFTEEN

APPY Valentine's Day! Oh, you all look so
sweet. I feel a diabetic coma coming on, you
all look so sweet. You two, stop necking and listen
to my routine. Does your mother know you're
here, honey? I'm gonna call her right now.
[*Brrinng*] HELLO? I THOUGHT YOU SHOULD KNOW
YOUR DAUGHTER IS HERE SLOBBERING ALL
OVER SOME YOUNG MAN. HM? JUST A MOMENT.
Are you a doctor? NO, HE'S NOT A DOCTOR. HM?
JUST A MOMENT. Are you a lawyer? NO, HE'S NOT
A LAWYER, EITHER. [*Slam*] She says get the hell
home.

Have you all made your New Year's resolutions? Have you *kept* your resolutions? Tsk, tsk. I
have. I resolved not to eat liver, drink motor oil or
grow my nose hair.

How many of you here are married? C'mon, this
is not a difficult thing, we raise our hands like so
. . . thank you. All you married ladies out there,
did you have white weddings? Hm? Did you dress
your bridesmaids like tarts? Aha! Nervous laughter. You did, you *did* dress them like tarts and you
did it on purpose. It's the VE Factor, isn't it? Hm?
Virginal Enhancement. If your attendants look
like tarts, *you* guys look like positive princesses! I
think it's rotten. To float down the aisle in a long
white gown behind three floosies in slit-to-there
fuchsia! Anyone would look good after that! The

groom's going, OH, MY GOD, HER FRIENDS ARE HOOKERS, then, AH, MY BRIDE!

Well, I'm single and I love it. [Break down in tears] No, I really do. I do all the right things. I treat myself right. For instance, just because you live alone doesn't mean you can get sloppy. You should treat yourself like a special guest. All the magazines say it. IF YOU AREN'T GOOD TO YOUR-SELF NO ONE ELSE WILL BE. So I try to be good to me. Last Valentine's Day, for instance, I washed my hair, I put on my best dress and I took myself out to a lovely restaurant for dinner. Then I told myself I was leaving me. I was furious! I knew I'd only taken me to a fancy restaurant so I wouldn't make a scene! Well, it didn't work. I threw wine in my lap and slapped my face.

Working on the streets and getting the odd private party was great. I could feel myself getting better and better. An idea would come to me on the street and I'd work on it and work on it and use it at a party. You could improvise a fair bit at parties, but it was better to have a set routine because the suggestions could get pretty obnoxious. If you asked them for a topic, for example, they almost always came up with toilets, brothels and mud wrestling. Over-originality. So when I got the dance in Guelph I decided not to give the students a chance to call out anything. I'd give them an act.

And what an act.

I put together another Sonny and Cher outfit, this time half suit and half bikini top and wispy long skirt. I used the same old half-and-half wig. I put a screen on stage and made my changes *very* quickly behind it. I basically did their lives from

"I Got You Babe" to Mayor of Palm Springs and Oscar. I even gave birth to Chastity on stage. It was a riot. When I turned for Sonny's side I'd kneel.

Ron and Kathy came to see me in Guelph. That was the first time any of my family had come to see me do anything. They were blown away. We went out for coffee after. Kathy was teary.

"Hey, don't cry just because I made fun of your idol."

"That's not it and you know it. My baby sister is good!"

"You really were, Kim," Ron said. "You were good. And I don't even like Cher." Kathy hit his arm.

"But enough about me. How's Deb?"

"Big."

"She's due any day now," Kathy said.

"We're going to be aunties," I said. The topic got on to babies and stuff and I drifted a little. It's awful but I could have talked about the act all night. When they dropped me off at my bus, they each tried to give me money. I didn't take it that time. I said I'd tap them for some when the time came.

It came soon enough. The nice guy from Book City told me about a club in the States called Hardcore Comedy. It was in New Jersey but he said tons of people trekked from Manhattan to see new acts and Wednesday night was amateur night. Everyone got a chance to try their stuff for a few minutes.

Once I'd heard about it, I was obsessed. I had to go. Silvy borrowed a car and drove me to the Buffalo airport.

"I think you're great doing this."

"Or stupid."

"C'mon, Red, you're excited."

"Yeah."

"Remember, if Carson is there, I'm your manager."

"Who's getting romantic now?"

"It's catching."

Why wouldn't I hit it big in the States? Hadn't it happened to Michael J. Fox? To the SCTV guys? To The Kids in the Hall? I was practically destined to continue a tradition. Wow them at Hardcore, get my Green Card and the world would be my oyster.

We'd left Toronto at seven a.m. to make an eleven o'clock flight. Silvy'd drawn the route in a yellow line on the map and I was supposed to navigate. I couldn't help thinking of the time Skye and I went shopping in Niagara Falls. It was about the last thing we ever did together.

When we crossed over from Canada to the States, Silvy put her cap on. She looked the picture of innocence.

"Where were you born?"

"Toronto." That wasn't true. Silvy told me she was born in England.

"Where were you born?"

"Humbilton, Hamilton, Ontario."

"How long will you be in the States?"

"Just for the day."

He waved us through. About a mile down the road Silvy took off her cap. As soon as we hit Stateside there were potholes like crazy. Silvy was handling the driving very well.

"How much driving have you done?" I asked.

"Hardly any." I grabbed onto the seat and door handle.

"Lemme outta here!"

"You just navigate."

There wasn't a lot of navigating to do, really. Before long there were big signs saying Buffalo International Airport. I went from excited to almost throwing up when I saw the planes landing.

"You've never been on a plane? Ever?" she asked.

"Nope."

"It's too bad your first experience has to be Continental Airlines."

"Why?"

"It's the old People's Express."

"And?"

"Let's just say it's not the Concorde." I was getting nervous. "You'll be fine. I've taken it lots of times."

"I wish you could come with me."

"Me, too."

"Why don't we run off to New York and become actors?"

"How much are you paying for your room, Red?"

"You know how much. Three hundred. Why?"

"You know what you'd get in New York for that?"

"What?"

"An elevator shaft, maybe."

"But the pay is better, right?

"Don't kid yourself. There's a saying. Even if you're one in a million, in New York there's seven more people just like you."

"How do people live there, then?"

"It's like the flight of the bumblebee. Aerodynamically impossible. Anyway, you're not going to New York. You're going to New Jersey."

"Yeah, but they're close."

"Only geographically."

"Turn here."

"I saw it."

There was an air park where you could leave your car and get it when you came back, but Silvy had to have the car back before two, so she just dropped me off.

"Nervous?"

"You're not kidding."

"You'll be great." She gave me a big hug. "Knock 'em dead, Red!"

She honked as she drove off and I stood there watching her until she disappeared. A bus pulled up that had brought people from the air park so I got caught up in their little wave and followed them into the airport. I'd never been to one before so I just kept asking people where to go. I found the Continental Airlines desk. There was a huge lineup and I got at the end of it. People were restless and angry-looking and I figured it was because of the lineup. Then I looked at the board behind the counter.

There was a CANCELLED sign beside Flight 307 to Newark.

What? Oh, my God. Well, I'd allowed myself tons of time. I'd just get on the next flight. Some of the men were getting obnoxious. One guy with a briefcase broke out of the line and stomped up to one of the girls.

"I have a meeting to get to. It's very important."

"Ahm sorry, sir," the girl kept saying, but he

made such a fuss that someone finally came and got him and took him to another airline. This got the rest of us, who were waiting our turn, even hotter under the collar. I thought of marching up and saying, "I have a comedy club to get to," but I didn't think they'd be impressed. Those girls, all about my age, had the most expressionless faces I'd ever seen. But when you got up to the desk, as I finally did, you could see their hands shaking as they keyed stuff in on the computer.

This was more stressful than scraping pasta off plates, that's for sure.

"Can I get on the next flight, please?"

"Ahm sorry, all flights are booked, m'am." I liked being called m'am.

"But I have to be in New Jersey tonight."

"You c'n go on stanbah."

"Standby! I'll go on standby!" She started to punch something in on the computer with her trembling fingers. "Will I get a seat soon?"

"Not tuhdaee, no m'am," she said, still keying in. But I *had* to get out. Wednesday was amateur night. Besides, Silvy was halfway home!

"I have to get out today! I have a very important meeting!" I don't think she bought that.

"Ahm sorry, m'am, there's nuthin' ah c'n dooo."

I was about to leap across the counter and strangle her, when a man in a brown uniform came over.

"Piedmont can take ten, but only ten," he said. I could hardly believe my luck.

"Oh, please, please," I said. "Let me go with Piedmont. You can have my firstborn child!" She didn't smile.

"Certainly, m'am. Ah'll put you on Peedmahnt."

She keyed in something and I found myself, along with nine grumps, following the guy in uniform. I was so happy.

I can't say my first airplane ride was a thrill — the packages of peanuts were awfully small — but I was just glad to have got a seat. What would I have done? I'd have been stranded at Buffalo Airport probably the very day that Carson and Letterman had decided to pop into Hardcore Comedy.

SIXTEEN

STANDING in the wings at Hardcore was my first taste of the real stuff. Yuk Yuks wasn't like this. All of us were nervous and all of us expected to be snapped up by some big agent and made into a star.

I felt sorry for the first three who'd gone up. The audience didn't even snicker. In fact, they barely listened. When this happened the lights were turned off on you and you had to leave the stage. But the fourth guy got their attention. He did it by going all quiet, whereas the first three might've been on something they were so wired. He finished his full one and a half minutes. Things were looking up.

There were more girls than I'd have expected. They did a lot of girl humour — menstruation, pantyhose. The lights flickered on them a lot. But it was mostly guys. A few you could tell had done this before but lots were clearly first-timers. The audience was pretty warmed up by about an hour into it and there were five guys ahead of me still to go.

After my first Yuk Yuks time in Humbletown I realized the value of a warmed-up audience. I'd rather have gone after someone who was good than someone who'd brought the lights down. By the time it got to two guys in front of me I was completely unaware of the routine. My ears felt like they were popping and my stomach had grabbing pains like I had the flu.

The emcee was on stage.

"Good routine. Was the unzipped fly part of it? Just kidding. Okay, let's welcome to open-mike night at Hardcore, Kimberly Taylor!"

Oh, my God, I thought, just jump right in. It's only one and a half minutes. If you're lucky.

"I'm not here to amuse you this evening. I've come on very serious business." It went all quiet. I'd intended to blast it out like a telethon but I learned from that third guy to draw them in. Now I was glad I hadn't been one of the first. It was good to have others out there ahead of you. Like shark bait. They were chuckling.

"That's right, the Adopt-a-Canadian Program." Laughter, glorious laughter. "Your dollars can help!" More laughter. "Friends, just 1.2 million can keep a Canadian family of four fed and clothed for a year." Big laugh. "Imagine the quiet joy you will feel as you receive pictures of your Canadians in their Ralph Laurens." They were loving it. "Bask in the knowledge that your contribution puts food on the table of a people who cannot even *spell* radicchio." They were going nuts. "And that's not all. Through your generous contribution, a Canadian family will be able to dream that impossible dream, reach for that unreachable star. Yes, your dollars will make it possible for a Canadian family to be what they have always wanted to be. Americans!" Thunderous laughter and applause. "Please give so that Canadians can really, really live!"

They were going nuts. I could have stayed there forever. When I got off the other side of the stage, a woman with tons of makeup took my arm.

"Great, hon. Down there."

I went down a narrow set of stairs. At the end

102

of a green hall was a room, and I could hear all kinds of commotion coming from it.

This must be where she wanted me to go. Sure enough, when I opened the door, all the comics who had managed to get through without being flickered off were there. They cheered me when I got in.

"You made it!"

"Way to go!"

There was some back-slapping and handshaking and before I knew it another guy had come through the door and I was cheering him along with the rest of them. Then, after about five minutes, we realized no one was coming through the door. The room went really quiet. What had happened?

There was complete silence as we all just stood there crowded together in the room.

"Und now vee turn on ze showerz."

"Tasteless, Herbie, totally tasteless."

It *was* tasteless, but I secretly agreed with Herbie. It was scary. Why was it so quiet? Was the audience dead?

"Our luck, this is the night they drop the bomb."

"Yeah, probably the one night a major agent comes to this dive."

"The only survivors, thirty comics in the basement of a sleazy club."

"We'll create a new civilization!"

"Better get started now!" Herbie said, grabbing me. He *was* funny. And he kissed me. It wasn't what I'd imagined, being kissed in a crowded basement room by a guy way shorter than me. But there was no terrace handy and Brad was far away. I kissed him back.

"Was it good for you?" Herbie said. I started sucking on an imaginary cigarette. He laughed. It might've got awkward and embarrassing, for me, anyway — Herbie was shameless — but a woman came through the door just then. We all practically jumped at her.

"Yay!"

"Well done!"

"You made it, momma!"

"What happened? Are they dead up there?"

This woman, who had a little extra weight on her, was hyperventilating.

"After you," she said, pointing to the last guy who'd come through the door, "they went dead. The guy ahead of me actually leaped on the front table and started CPR."

"What happened?"

"They doused him."

"So what did you do, momma?"

"I stood on my head."

"No kidding!"

"Yeah. By the time I got my legs straight my time was up!"

A few moments later another girl came through the door and we made the same fuss over her.

"You warmed them up," she said to the woman. The woman was still having trouble breathing and was red in the face. I hoped I'd never get so desperate for a laugh that I'd stand on my head at that age. But it worked, so what the heck.

"What are we doing here?" I asked Herbie. He and I were sort of acquainted, after all.

"Waiting for the agents."

"Agents? Really? You mean they really come here?"

"Sure. What'd you think, just mommies and daddies out front?" He had an accent. He said "shoowa" instead of "sure." Of course the fantasy of agents had sustained me for years. But what would I do if I actually met one?

"My agent's a dickhead," Herbie said.

"You have an agent?"

"Sure." *Shoowa*.

"Then why are you waiting here?"

"'Cause he don't get me work. I got a friend? His agent gets him something every week. I don't care if it's a wedding, he gets him something. You know where my friend is now?" I shook my head. "Catch a Rising Star." *Stah*. Even I'd heard of that. Herbie looked me in the eyes. For a laugh-a-minute guy, he was very serious. "Get a good agent. That's my advice."

The door opened and the woman with the makeup came in. Everyone was on edge. She had a small pile of business cards in her hand.

"Twenty-one," she called out, and the tall guy who'd done fish impersonations screamed and came forward.

"Seven." This was a girl. She burst into tears when her number was called. It didn't take a math whiz to see there wasn't a card for every one of us.

"Twenty-one." The fish guy again. Two agents interested. Wow.

"Fifty-two." The room was quiet.

"Fifty-two?" Hey! That was me! That pounding was going on in my ears again. I got the card from the woman who didn't call me hon or anything this time. She just kept calling out numbers. I could hardly believe it. I just kept staring at the card.

Susan Greer
Mather & Roszinski
Talent Agents

And at the bottom there were two phone numbers — one for Toronto and one for New York.

I was holding onto the card with two hands, just staring at it. What was I supposed to do? Would someone be upstairs waiting for me? Would we have a drink at the bar and discuss contracts? What was I supposed to do?

"Shit! Canada!" This was from Herbie. He'd only got one card and it was Susan's. But there was a New York number on it, too. So why not have a New York-Canada connection?

He told me why not.

"I know this guy? He went to Toronto. Ended up marrying some schoolteacher. He's living in Scarberia, man, with a bunch of screaming kids at his feet. Tor-on-toe makes you *clean*, man, sucks the juices out. You start wanting things like Peace and Qui-yet. You start saying 'eh' and watching freaking hockey games." But I noticed he put the card in his hip pocket.

The room had pretty well emptied out. The older woman hadn't got a card, which was too bad since she'd got the crowd back.

"Never mind. Some day my card will come."

"You've done this before?"

"You kidding? Every week! I live on Clinton." I gathered we were close to Clinton. I'd just asked the taxi driver to take me to Hardcore. It was hard to imagine doing open-mike night every week.

"Now what am I supposed to do?" I asked her.

Herbie had taken off, or I'd have asked him. I guessed we weren't destined to be buddies.

"You go home and you phone Ms. Greer."

We got up the stairs and the club was completely empty. No one was hanging around to buy me a drink.

"Where is everybody" I asked.

"What do you think, they're gonna wait around and congratulate us? Nah, they go on to the next club. Head over to Manhattan. The night is young."

It was one o'clock in the morning.

SEVENTEEN

A T three-thirty a.m. I was standing in Newark International Airport. The lights of Manhattan were beckoning to me.

I got a little clutch in my stomach. Being famous meant being known by everyone in New York. Everyone. On the ride back to the airport I'd been thinking that. Famous is having the taxi driver know who you are. And every person in every highrise. You say the name Kim Taylor and they go, oh, yeah. They know you.

There was a bus that would take me to Manhattan from the airport for less than ten bucks. I'd have loved to have got on it, but Silvy would be waiting for me in Buffalo at eight-thirty. Providing the flight wasn't cancelled.

"You're a Leo." I turned and saw a woman in a long dress with long grey hair. "And your name begins with, don't tell me . . ." She closed her eyes. " . . . K."

"That's amazing," I said. She leaned close and put her hand on my arm and squeezed it.

"You're going to be famous, Leo. Careful what you wish." Then she kind of glided off. She was right about the first two points. Why not the third? I looked around the airport. Famous would be having all these people know who you are. Every one.

There was no way I could sleep. I still hadn't come down from the Hardcore, but I saw an empty space on one of the couches and decided to take it. Some couch. It was like an elongated version of

108

the vinyl office furniture back in my room. This is how Silvy had spent so much of her time, sleeping in airports.

When I sat down a girl with short black hair and a leather jacket stretched and opened her eyes.

"Sorry, did I wake you up?"

"Not really," she yawned. "I was just dozing." She sat up and stretched her face. She actually stretched her face. Her eyes went all wide and her mouth opened as far as it could go and she stretched her face. Then she burst out laughing.

"I was doing it, wasn't I?"

"What?" She did her face again.

"That."

"Yeah."

"It's a habit. I can't help myself. Be careful, it's catching."

"Really?" I couldn't imagine why.

"Yeah. So, where are you going?"

"Buffalo. Then Toronto."

"No kidding! Me, too. Continental?"

"Yeah."

"Me, too! You got a ride?"

"Yeah."

"I'll come with you, okay?"

"Sure." What did I say that for? For all I knew she was a murderer. A serial murderer who stretched her face before she sliced up her victims.

"I'm getting the seven-thirty flight, though," I said, kind of hoping she'd be on a different one.

"Of course. It's the only one that's sure not to be cancelled." I just looked at her. "The plane's been here all night. It's guaranteed to leave. It's the only one I ever take."

"I get it."

"What you do, if you can't make the seven-thirty, you book three flights. If you get on the first one you cancel the two others. Gina Delrisio."

"Kim Taylor." We shook hands.

"You from Toronto?"

"Yeah." I almost said No, Hamilton.

"I'm from Hamilton."

"*What*?"

"What?"

"This is bizarre. *I'm* from Hamilton!"

"You said Toronto."

"I just moved there. I grew up in Hamilton!"

"Really? Where?"

"Chatham Street." She didn't know it. "Off Dundurn. Near the liquor store."

"Oh, yeah, yeah. What're you doing here?" I told her. "You're a comic? God, that's great. I know a comedian!" We shook hands again.

"What're you doing?"

"Oh, I been travelling around. You know, this and that."

"You been to New York?"

"Manhattan? Yeah, I just came from there."

"What's it like?"

"A zoo. Awful. Well, some things are fun. If you meet some nice people you get a nice meal, maybe go to a club, hear some good comedy." She was elbowing me. "But most of the time it's just a stinkin' zoo."

We didn't sleep a wink, of course, and by the time we touched down in Buffalo I'd been awake more than twenty-four hours. Silvy was happy to meet Gina and had no problems with dropping her off in Toronto. I knew she wouldn't. Silvy

110

wanted to hear all about it and I told her every excruciating detail even though Gina was there.

"An agent? Let me see the card." I pulled out Susan Greer's card. "Did you call?"

"Not yet. It was three a.m."

"Call from my place."

"Okay, thanks."

"Well, Red, I guess I'm not going to be your manager after all."

"I'm sorry."

"Oh, don't be a nut case. This is terrific! We've got to celebrate. A party!" Oh, great. The last thing I needed was a party. "Jeremy's been bugging me about you."

"*Jeremy?*"

"Yeah."

"That was ages ago."

"I think he was otherwise entangled at the time."

"Oh, my God."

"Face it, Red, your life is starting to happen."

I leaned back and stretched my face. Gina was right. It was catching.

EIGHTEEN

"**O**PERATOR."

"I'd like to hold for time and charges, please."

"Certainly."

Silvy slapped my arm, but I'd learned that from my mother. It seemed like forever before the phone rang. Then it rang twice before it was picked up. I was holding my breath.

"Hello, this is Susan Greer. Let's not play telephone tag. Leave your name and number after the beep and I'll get back to you as soon as I can."

"Um. Ahem. Hi. Hello, Susan. It's Kim Taylor calling. You left me your card at Hardcore Comedy Club the other night? I'm just calling — "
Beep.

"Oh, God, did you hear that?" I said to Silvy. "I can't even leave a decent message. She'll think I'm a complete twit."

"One minute, a dollar-ten." Right. I guess I thought I'd be having a ten-minute chat with my agent.

"Thank you." I hung up. "Oh, gee, what a dork."

"Kim, it wasn't an audition. Call her Toronto number."

"Right."

I called, but Susan wasn't in, although they expected her the next day, so I left my name and Silvy's number since I still only had the pay phone in the hall. There was no point in calling New York again if she was coming to Toronto anyway.

Agent. What a magical word. Silvy kept saying,

112

"You'll have to check that with your agent," and "Kim's agent is coming to town tomorrow."

The day passed so slowly, even though we had fun taking Gina around looking for a job. Her travel money had run out and that's why she came back to Canada. Gina was the second person to sign my wall. She was going to stay at Silvy's house for awhile. That was fine by the others.

Around five o'clock I fell asleep on Silvy's couch. Every so often I'd hear the door open and shut and people coming and going, but I was so pooped I couldn't open my eyes, much less lift my head up. No one minded. They were used to strange people turning up in that house, and it's not like they didn't know me. When I did wake up it was one a.m. I was all turned around. Silvy was just coming in off her shift. That familiar Spaghetti Factory smell wafted toward me. I sat up.

"How was it?"

"Same as ever."

"That bad? When are you going to quit that place?"

"Soon." I looked at her. She was looking mischievous.

"Really? Soon?"

"Yeah. I've saved some money and . . . I've got a part in a play."

"What? Silvy! That's fabulous! Why didn't you tell me? What play? When did you hear? When did you audition?"

"Remember the part I auditioned for last summer?" I nodded but I didn't remember. She'd probably told me but I was too caught up in the street thing. "Well, I didn't get that one. But I got

113

a call to audition for another play by the same guy and I got it!"

"When did you hear?"

"Tonight. They called me at work."

"Oh, Silvy, that's great." I gave her a hug.

We went out for a hamburger to celebrate, even though Silvy'd been up almost twenty-four hours. We were revved.

"Where is it going to be?"

"Bathurst Street Theatre."

"Who's the guy?"

"Mark Hannon. He's really cute."

"Oh, I see."

"Now stop that. Nothing's happened. Yet."

"What happened to 'the world's biggest disappointment?'"

"Did I say that?"

"Mhm."

"Well, you know what they say. Hope springs eternal."

"I've never heard anyone say that, Silvy." She giggled. This was a new Silvy. Was it love? Where was all that cynicism I'd come to rely on?

"So what about you and Jeremy?"

"What about me and Jeremy?"

"C'mon, Kim, go out with the guy. What would it hurt?"

"You like Jeremy?" She thought for a second mid chew.

"He's a bit of an egghead. But he seems nice."

"Right."

"Besides, he'd be good for your first. Older. Undemanding."

"Silvy!"

"Oh, c'mon, Red, get it over with! You can't be a famous comedian and a virgin."

Famous comedian. Famous. But what if I became famous and Brad saw me and gave me a call and we got together for an elegant dinner, and he realized he'd always cared for me. Wouldn't it be nice to have waited for Brad?

"Oh, my God, it's him again, isn't it?" Silvy was giving me a disgusted look.

"Who?"

"The preppie guy. You've got the moonlit terrace look in your eyes again." I shrugged. "Face it, Red, the guy's a creep. He bought the lies about you and he trashed you to your friends."

"But if he found out the truth, he'd realize what I'd gone through and he'd spend the rest of his life making it up to me."

"Kim. If he ever finds out the truth, which he won't, he'll spend the rest of his life trying to make it up to Skye, which he can't." She was piling empty creamers on her tray and wiping her hands furiously with a napkin. "You're eighteen — "

"Seventeen," I interrupted.

"You're almost eighteen. I'm calling Jeremy tomorrow and asking him to the goodbye party for Lucy. And you're coming, too." I rolled my eyes.

"Wait a minute. What about Lucy?"

"She's going to Japan."

"Japan?"

"Yeah. She's going to teach English and save lots of yen." Silvy sat back. "Lucy's going to Japan and Gina's moving into her room and I figure I'll get Gina in my old job at the Spaghetti Factory. I'm going to work on my craft. And you, Humble-

115

town, are going to become a famous comedian. But first you have to lose your status as a GTV."

"You've certainly got my life all planned."

"Hey, I was supposed to be your manager."

Silvy was just one of the people in my life at that time who figured they knew what was best for me.

NINETEEN

"**S**TAND up."

I stood up. Susan Greer walked slowly around me. I followed her part way with my eyes. "Where do you get your clothes?"

"Salvation Army, Goodwill . . ."

"That's got to stop."

"It won't be easy. Once you've paid a dollar-fifty for a shirt, it's hard to go to ten."

She didn't laugh.

Susan was not my fantasy of a motherly agent at all. She was young and tough and she looked like a lawyer. Her office would've looked like a law office, too, if not for the pictures. Glossy pictures all over one wall.

"You've got talent, Kim." Ah, she said it at last. "You know what talent counts for in this business?" I raised my eyebrows. I was thinking talent was everything in this business. "Two percent." *Two percent*? "Two percent talent, ten percent presentation and eighty-eight percent sweat."

"Sweat?"

"Hard work. I can help you with presentation — "

"Is that why you take ten percent?" The corners of her mouth didn't even turn up.

"Fifteen. I take fifteen percent."

"Right."

"I can help you with presentation, and I will, and if you're smart you'll take my advice. But all the talent and presentation in the world can't help someone who won't work. You understand?"

"Yes." I didn't tell her it had been a piece of cake so far. You go out on the streets and do what you feel like and if people like you they put a dollar in your hat and if they don't they keep walking. No problem.

"No more street stuff."

"What?"

"No more street stuff. I'm grooming you for clubs."

"But . . ." She looked at me. She looked like a teacher more than a lawyer then. I guess she wouldn't be too interested in hearing how much fun it was. How I'd met Jesus and how I had my regulars and how much I'd learned.

"You've learned all you can on the streets." *She reads minds, too.* "It's time to move on. Clubs are where it's at. You know how many club dates Jay Leno does a year?" I shook my head. "Two hundred and fifty." *Two hundred and fifty? He must be nuts!* "Two hundred and fifty one-nighters a year. You think of him as a Johnny substitute, right? Well, you only see the very tip of the iceberg. Those two hundred and fifty one-nighters are what keep him on top." I didn't know what to say because while I knew who Jay Leno was, I'd never seen him. But she was waiting for me to say something so I tried for another joke.

"I'll bet *he* doesn't get heckled."

"If you can't take the hecklers, Kim, get out now." *Geez, it was just a joke.*

"I can take them." She looked at me.

"You were an unpopular kid, right?" Well, she got that one. At least I was until Skye. "Right? All you comics are the same." *All us comics?*

"Right."

118

"So use that. Remember what it was like to have your nose made fun of, your freckles, your skinny legs, your flat chest." *You want a punch in the chops, Sue baby?* "Because the hecklers will. They'll use it. They're not very original."

"I've noticed that."

"So get them. Now's your opportunity to tell Billy or Sally from the fourth grade what you really think of them. It's what a club audience loves, you know. It's like watching a trapeze artist without a net. You think they come to hear your clever routine, but they really come to see you fall flat on your face. But if you can put down the fat guy in the back, they're with you. They love you." She went over to her desk and picked up a couple of stapled papers. "This is a standard contract. Take it away, look at it. Do you know a lawyer?" I nodded. There was my mum's boss, even though I'd only met him a couple of times. "Have her look at it if you want. The sooner you sign, the sooner I'll get you working." I was ready to sign right then but she obviously didn't expect that, unlike at Stagewise, which is another way I had of telling she was for real.

We stood there looking at each other. There was nothing more to say until I signed on, so I left. No motherly hugs. No "You'll-be-fine-dear."

The reception area was really small, and I'd had to have been blind to miss the guy waiting outside Susan's office.

"Herbie!" He looked up and smiled.

"Hey . . ."

"Kim."

"Kim! How ya doin'? You got Susan's card?"

"Yeah. I thought you weren't interested in Tor-

119

ron-toe." He looked at the closed door, then back at me. Then he leaned in and talked in a low voice.

"I wasn't. But this Greer chick is a woman after my own heart."

"Why didn't you see her in New York, then?"

"There *is* no New York office." He was positively gleeful. "She says to me she says, 'You can leave thirty messages in Toronto and not get a call back, but you leave a New York number and they phone the same day.' Ha! She's only got an *answering* machine in New York. My kind of woman!"

"You can go in now, Herbie," the receptionist said.

"Catch you later, Duchess," Herbie said, and then he opened the door to Susan's office and said, "I'm here!" in a loud voice. Once he'd closed the door I couldn't hear anything. The receptionist smiled and shrugged. I got the elevator.

Duchess? Why Duchess? And how was he going to catch me later? He didn't ask for my phone number. I didn't *have* a phone number. I was beginning to think a phone was maybe something I should have.

On the way home I caught sight of myself in a store window. Black T-shirt, black jeans. I'd been dressing this way since I was fifteen. It would be hard to stop. And expensive.

"No, no," Silvy said when I called her, "I'll help you. You just need a couple of stage outfits. The rest of the time you can wear whatever you want."

"Stage outfits?"

"Yeah. I see you in a green sequined vest over tuxedo pants. And tails. You should have tails. We'll go to this store on Queen Street. Gina will help. She sews, too."

"You really like Gina, eh?"

"I like all you girls from Humbletown."

"Did she get your job?"

"Better. She's going to be cooking the slop."

"You're kidding."

"Nope. So when do we go shopping?"

"I have to have someone look at the contract first. Even Susan said so."

"Kimberly, sign."

"I'm going to have my mum's boss look at it."

"You're a nutcase. An agent from New York hands you a — "

"She's not from New York. She just has an answering machine so people from Toronto will return her calls."

"Hey, she sounds like a go-getter."

"That's what Herbie said."

"*Her*bie? *Her*bie? Who's Herbie?"

"This guy. He was at Hardcore. Hoibie."

"Bring Hoibie to the party. You'll have two guys to choose from. Hey, Red, you're not as slow as you look."

"Thanks."

"Get that contract signed."

She hung up. I realized I hadn't asked her a thing about the play. Oh, well, I'd get to that. Everyone sure thought I should sign on with Susan. Even mum's boss said, "This is a pretty standard contract, Kim. I have no problems with it. Congratulations." So I signed.

Why didn't I feel fantastic? This was what a lot of people would kill for. A contract with an agent who had an answering machine in New York. Is everything always a let-down once you get it?

TWENTY

THE second I signed on with Susan Greer, she had me booked into a club. It was nothing like Yuk Yuks. It was really nothing like the private parties for my regulars. No one was listening.

There I was on a tiny stage in my old black stuff because there'd been no time to put anything together. No one laughed. No one listened. I had a new routine, too — about airlines since now I was an expert — but I could barely hear myself talk. After my set I went to the bar for my money. The big bartender just looked at me.

"My money, please," I practically had to scream.

"What for?"

"My routine."

"Did you take your clothes off?"

Everyone at the bar laughed. The first laugh of the night. My cheeks must've been blazing red.

"My comedy routine," I said.

"Oh, you *did* take your clothes off." Another big laugh from the bar.

Finally he took a fifty out of the tin and handed it to me. I called a taxi because I was scared to walk to the subway. Scared in case one of the jerks from the bar followed me out. So when I counted my taxi money and took off fifteen percent for Susan, I'd cleared around twelve dollars that night. Twelve dollars to stand up and not be listened to. Twelve dollars to be made fun of at the bar. Twelve dollars to be scared out of my wits. When I got back to my little room and looked at my stickman curtains, I just let go and cried. I cried and cried and didn't bother getting undressed. The only good part was that no one I knew had been there. I cried myself to sleep.

Two nights later I had another club date, and this time Susan was going to be in the audience. I decided I would do my crowd-pleasing Sonny and Cher imitation. When I walked out in my half-and-half outfit, it got their attention. For awhile. Halfway through "I Got You Babe," they got bored. No one clapped or joined in like they had on the street. They started to turn to each other and talk. I could feel it starting to get louder and louder like it had the other night in the first club. Once that happened, there was no getting them back. I felt like crying, but I just kept singing.

Midway through "The Beat Goes On," a voice called out, "Hey, Cher, you can't sing." It was a woman's voice. A familiar woman's voice. It was Susan. What was I supposed to say to that? I just kept on going with the routine.

"Hey, Cher," the voice said again, "you can't sing." A few people started to pipe down like they were getting interested. Only they were looking at Susan, not me. I knew this was a test, but I was frozen. She said it again. Now they were mostly quiet. I turned my Cher side to the audience.

"Hey, Sonny, did you hear that? She said I can't sing." I turned my Sonny side to the audience and got down on my knees.

"I've been saying that for years, Cher." This got a little chuckle.

"Oh, yeah?" I was Cher again. "Well, you can't sing and you can't act, and you're short." This got a laugh, but now I was stuck again. I was stuck in a Sonny and Cher argument. So I improvised — got a divorce, married Greg Allman, divorced him, then won an Oscar. But I was stuck with this Sonny half of me and so I couldn't face the audience or turn the other side to them. I felt them slipping away again. Losing interest.

"Hey, Cher." Susan again. "I thought you got rid of Sonny."

"Well, you know how it is. He'll always be a part of me." Not even a chuckle.

"I think he's your better half." Big laugh. Great. My agent was getting the laughs. My heckling agent. Then the audience started in, only they weren't as bright as Susan. They got personal.

"Hey, Cher, your nose is big."

"Show us your tattoo."

I could feel my lower lip start to go. All I could do to keep myself together was finish the act. It seemed like it took forever, but I know it was only a few minutes.

When I scrambled off I went straight to the backstage bathroom and got into my own clothes. And I scrubbed off all the makeup. I looked about twelve. A tall twelve. Sometimes I could look thirty and sometimes I could look twelve. I slapped on a little lip gloss and combed out my hair. And I caught myself stretching my face. Why did it feel so good? I packed my costume in my suitcase.

If only I didn't have to go out there.

I made my way out front and sat at the bar waiting for Susan. There was no one on stage. It was a break between me and the singer.

"Hey, cutie, goin' my way?"

"Leave her alone, Al," the bartender said. It was a woman this time. "Want a Coke, sweetie?"

124

I nodded. When she handed it to me she said, "You lookin' for someone?" That's when it hit me. They didn't recognize me! I thought it would be painful having to walk out front after that fiasco, but no one knew who I was!

"How do you feel about it?" Susan was standing beside me.

"Sick."

"I've seen worse." That was the nicest thing she'd ever said to me. "The impersonation was good, but the costume limits you."

"Right."

"Why did you freeze?"

"Hm?"

"When they started with the insults. Why did you freeze?"

"Well, I wanted to answer them in character."

"Why?" I couldn't think why. I just knew I did. "You're not an actress, Kim, you're a comedian. You're in control up there. You're on your own. If you're good it's because of you and if you're bad it's because of you." She took a sip of her drink. "You know why I think you froze?"

"Why?"

"It's the Canadian thing. You're too polite. That's why I like working with Americans. You know Herbie?"

"Yeah."

"He's not afraid to zap the crowd. In fact, he loves it. I'm going to help him with his presentation and he's already been sweating. You know Herbie's only problem?" I shook my head. "No talent." She tapped my arm. "You've got talent, Kim. But, hey, it's only two percent." She got me my money from the bartender and took her cut. "Call

my office in a few days for your next club date."
She stood up. "And Kim." I was thinking she'd
maybe end with a little inspirational message.

"Yeah?"

"Work on the outfit." Then she left.

"Is that your mother?" the bartender asked.

"No. My agent."

"You're an actress?"

"Not really." She was waiting for an explanation
but I was too pooped. Susan had paid for my Coke
so I grabbed my suitcase and started to leave. The
singer was on stage now. No one was listening to
her, either.

TWENTY-ONE

SILVY and Gina and I went to the store they knew on Queen and bought two pairs of tuxedo pants and a coat with tails. Then we went to a sewing store and bought green sequined material and a pattern for a vest. The material cost more than a pair of pants.

"It's an investment," they kept saying.

"What am I going to wear under the vest?"

"I don't think you should wear anything."

"Silvy!" Gina said. "She's not a Playboy bunny."

"I just think it would get their attention."

"I got their attention the other night with the Cher outfit. Lasted maybe thirty seconds." I told them all about it.

"God, I'm glad I wasn't there," Silvy said. "I'd have pounded Susan."

"She's just trying to help. She says my problem is I'm Canadian." They looked at each other.

"There's something to that," Gina said.

"Yeah, there's something to it," Silvy said.

We had a hoot working on my costume at Silvy and Gina's. We ordered in pizza and got it done in one session. I came downstairs in the pants and vest only and they applauded.

"Definitely wear it without anything underneath," Silvy said.

"I can't. My arms are too white."

"Wear makeup," Gina said.

"On my arms?"

"Sure."

I said I'd think about it. The fact is I couldn't

wear a white blouse because the sweat would show, and besides I'd have to wash it every ten seconds. I had a black leotard I figured I'd try.

The outfit did a weird thing to me on stage. I didn't have anything to hide behind anymore. It was just me out there.

One night I collected my money from the bartender and headed over to Bathurst Street Theatre where Silvy's play was going on. It wasn't starting till midnight. I slid into a seat in the middle of the opening comic's act. It was Marla Lukofski. She fascinated me. Most of the jokes were about her. Jokes about her nose, body hair, thighs, but she seemed angry most of the time. Angry at us. She was a lot like Herbie.

It came to me in a flash what was wrong with me. I was trying to make people laugh at something other than them or me. It's amazing that it took that long to get the message into my head. Susan had told me to watch Johnny Carson and count the jokes. Count how many were put-downs of the audience or Ed or guests. Gina and I had done this little bit of homework and were astounded that out of seventy-seven jokes, seventy-two were put-downs. Somehow I'd never really noticed that. Even the looks into the camera were really put-downs. And people *loved* Johnny. And they were loving Marla. The applause when she left the stage was bigger than anything I'd ever got, especially these days when I never got any. These days I was happy for some pity from the woman in the front row, never mind applause.

Of course, I couldn't keep my mind on the play. I was watching it and yet not watching it. I was watching it and simultaneously imagining my new act. I hardly noticed when someone sat beside me during intermission.

"Kim, right?"

"Herbie! What're you doing here?"

"I came to see Marla."

"She was good."

"Good? She's great." I didn't say anything. Okay, okay, she'd inspired me, but I didn't think she was great. "What're you doin' here?" *Heah*.

"My friend Silvy's in the show."

"Which one?"

"Pink hair."

"Not bad, not bad. Maybe you'll introduce me."

"Sure."

"I'll sit with you for the second half and you can introduce me to your friend, huh?"

I didn't say anything. The lights were going down. It was hard to follow the second act when I'd been drifting through the first. Also, Herbie's foot was going a mile a minute. He had his right foot resting on his left knee and he kept jiggling it the whole time. I sat in the dark trying to watch the play but all I could think about was how I'd have to be more like Marla and Herbie. I think the play was almost over before I realized my foot was jiggling, too. And worst of all, I was stretching my face.

TWENTY-TWO

SILVY'S house was a zoo, but it wasn't pulsating this time. There was a large theatre crowd, which in some ways was more nerve-racking than the university crowd. Lots of black clothes and red lipstick.

Herbie and I arrived together, but I was under no delusion that he was my date. Every ten seconds on the subway he had leaned in and said something like, "Would you look at *those*," or "I'd love to get my hands on *that*." Even when my brother Ron was at the height of the pubescent hornies, he'd never subjected me to so many ogling comments. I told Herbie so.

"Aw, Duchess, lighten up. Lighten up."

"What's with this Duchess stuff?"

"You know, red hair like that royal chick, what's 'er name."

"Fergie?"

"Yeah, Fergie. Duchess of York." Only he said "Eyawk." "And," he continued, "you got a kind of snotty way about you, ya know?"

"I beg your pardon?"

"Right. Like that. 'I beg your pardon.' Then you look down that nose at me like, 'Where did *it* come from?'" He leaned in. "You know, Duchess, you and me, we should get married. Think of what great kids we'd have! We could hang our laundry on their schnozes!"

The door opened. Gina was standing there.

"Kim!"

"Hi, Gina, this is — "

"Gina!" Herbie grabbed her and kissed her. "I'm Herbie. You were fabulous."

"I was?"

"She wasn't in the show, Herbie," I said.

"What? A good-lookin' girl like you? I've seen you in something, though, what was it? That perfume commercial, right? You're comin' through this wall of fire and you look at us and say — "

"I work in the Spaghetti Factory."

"No, no, it wasn't that. It was somethin' else."

Gina was laughing. The next thing I knew Herbie had his arm around her shoulders and was walking into the living room.

"Spaghetti Factory, huh? I'm told it's a very fine establishment." I saw Silvy in the kitchen and went to her. I gave her a big hug.

"You were wonderful!" I said, hoping she wouldn't ask me too much about the play.

"Thanks. Kim, this is Mark Hannon. He's the writer."

Mark and I shook hands. He was about my height with a frizzy ponytail and little round John Lennon glasses. I mumbled something about enjoying the play and he mumbled something back and Silvy pulled me into the hall.

"What do you think?"

"Of Mark?"

"Yeah."

"The glasses are a little hostile." She made a face. "But he seems nice. Really nice."

"And so talented."

"Clearly."

"Who's the guy you came in with?"

"Hoibie."

"Oh, *that's* Hoibie. I should meet him."

"Don't worry, you will. He'll see to that."

"He seems to like Gina."

"He likes goils, Silvy."

"Are you two . . . ?"

"No. We're friends."

"Good. Because Jeremy is here."

"Oh, God."

"Kim. Be nice." Right. I'd forgotten this was the new "isn't-Mark-wonderful" Silvy, not the old "men-are-one-big-disappointment" Silvy.

"How can I be anything else? I'm Canadian." She was looking over my shoulder.

"Here he comes. I'm going to disappear."

"Silvy."

"Ta-ta."

Ta-ta? Is that how we were talking now? Ta-ta?

"Kimberly?" I turned, and sure enough it was Jeremy looking pretty much the same as before. In fact, I think he was wearing the same jacket. "Remember me?"

"Of course I remember you, Jeremy. You saved me from a concussion." That's something that the clubs had taught me. You can be as cool as a cucumber on the outside no matter *how* you feel on the inside.

"Can I get you a drink?"

"No Black Russians."

"No Black Russians." I stood there with my hands in my pockets, but he was back soon. "I found some white wine." He handed me a glass.

"Thanks. I should be able to handle that." A few moments of awkward silence.

"Silvy tells me you're getting quite a bit of work."

"Yep."

"I'd like to come see you sometime."

"No, you wouldn't." He looked like I'd hit him. "I mean, when you're new, it's a pretty ugly scene. I've got a lot of time to put in before I want *anyone* to see me." He nodded.

"I can appreciate that." More awkward silence. For all his grossness, Herbie sure was easy to talk to. What did Mum used to say? Ask them about themselves.

"So, how are you? How's Poli Sci?"

His face lit up, and he proceeded to tell me. I felt like saying, "Listen, Jeremy, the last time you lectured me like this I had to get drunk to listen," but I didn't. I pretended to listen and I think I did quite well. I think I nodded in all the right places. After he wound down we both just stood there for a bit.

"I think I'm out of my depth here," Jeremy said. I knew what he meant. There was a heated argument in the kitchen about Brecht, and Herbie was centre stage in the living room with his arm still around Gina.

"I don't feel too comfortable here, either."

"Really?"

"Really. But at least I understand most of the words, whereas I don't have a clue what you were talking about." He laughed. He had a nice shy laugh.

"You want to go for a walk?"

"Sure."

"Should you tell that guy?"

"Herbie? No. Herbie's . . . just Herbie."

"But you came with him, didn't you?"

"Not really. He kind of attached himself to me at the theatre. He's a comic, too."

Jeremy and I left. Silvy gave me a thumbs-up sign as I headed for the door. What did she think? I was going to take him home with me? Sheesh.

We did a lot of walking and we stopped for coffee at the Second Cup. I must say it feels a lot safer having a guy with you. Even a tweedy guy. By the time we'd finished our coffee I'd heard all about this previous "entanglement" and how she'd been a very depressive person and how he had to ease out slowly for fear that she'd kill herself. I think the subtext was that a bouncy, up person like myself would be a relief after Jessica. That was her name. Jeremy and Jessica. That sounded nice. That would be hard to give up, all right. It would look so good on the wedding napkins.

"I'm not a reader, Jeremy." What an understatement.

"Hey, that's okay. I'm tired of readers. Jessica would sit with a Dickens all day." He got a little misty here. "I'd come in and she'd be in tears over the death of little Dombey." He was drifting on me.

"I've never read Dickens."

"Not one? Ever?"

"Not one. Now, I've seen 'A Christmas Carol' a million times. And 'Oliver.'"

"You don't read at all?"

"Nope. I start to and by the second paragraph I'm off in another world." I couldn't tell if he really disapproved of this. He claimed to find it a refreshing change from Jessica.

"But your knowledge of world events is astounding."

What a riot! He'd gone on for two hours about the Eastern Bloc and I wasn't even sure what that was. I'd only been nodding appropriately, and he thought *I* had a knowledge of world events. Because I listened to him! *Ladies — How to Catch and Hold a Man — hang on his every word. It works!*

It was five a.m. and we were standing outside the laundromat and I had no intention of inviting him up. He didn't push. He wasn't a pushy guy.

"May I see you again?" *I'd rather not.*

"Sure." He kissed me. He had these soft dry lips underneath the whiskers.

"Bye."

"Bye."

I went through the laundromat which smelled of fabric softener and made my way upstairs to my little room. I was so tired. I flopped on the bed without taking off my makeup. I fell asleep immediately, but it wasn't a restful sleep because it was full of dreams. Dreams of Brad.

TWENTY-THREE

"I LIKE the outfit, Kim. It works."

"Thanks." Susan sat across her desk from me with a cup of coffee.

"So. What is it you wanted to see me about?"

"I . . . just want to know how things are going. How I'm doing. What's next."

"You're doing great. You grossed five hundred dollars last month."

"What's next?"

"More of the same." I managed not to roll my eyes, but I couldn't stifle the sigh. "Look, Kim, this is what it's all about." *Oh, God, not the Jay Leno two-hundred-and-fifty-one-nighters-a-year talk again.* "I'm going to keep booking you into dives until you make them listen. Until someone calls me and says, 'Hey, that red-headed girl, we'd like her back. We'd like her for a week.'" I didn't say anything. I felt another sigh coming on. "You thought it would always be like Yuk Yuks in Hamilton?" *Wait a minute.*

"You were there?"

"I was there. The audience was full of nice moderately sober mums and dads. And you were cute." *She was there?* "I was amazed when I saw you at Hardcore. That took guts. Also, you were better. So I sent round my card." I just sat there kind of stunned. "Kim, I think you could be big. But big doesn't come from a lot of nice safe amateur nights. You could do Yuk Yuks for three or four years, get married, have a few kids and have this neat thing in your past to talk about and think about while you're washing dishes. *Or*, you could trust me, let me guide you to something more. For every overnight sensation, Kim, there's years of hard work to back them up."

"You think I could be big?"

She nodded.

"So do you."

Well, yeah, but I wanted to hear it from someone else. Someone besides the loco in Newark International Airport.

"Kim." She looked at her watch. "I'm not interested in being liked. I'm not a hand-holder. This is my business and I work hard at it. I see everything. I go to Yuk Yuks, Theatresports, the Old Firehall. I go to the dives and the clubs. I even go to high school comedy nights." *Really?*

"Did you see me on the streets?"

"Of course." I was waiting to hear how cute I was. "I'm interested in drive. I want to sign on people who want it. Want it more than anything in the world. Do you, Kim? Because that's what it takes."

I knew what "it" was. "It" was fame, and I wanted it. But more than anything in the world?

"Do you?"

"Yes."

"Then you'll get it." She looked at her watch again. I took the hint and stood up.

"Thanks, Susan."

"No problem."

I left. I pretended to myself that I'd had an uplifting talk with my kind-hearted agent. When I stepped out in the hall I opened my eyes and mouth as wide as I could. Face-stretching felt so good.

137

TWENTY-FOUR

THAT night in the sleazy club I was playing I decided to try the trick that had worked so well for the guy at Hardcore. I'd just be still and wait till I had their attention. I walked out onto the little black stage. No one looked at me. There were hoots of laughter from the bar. It hit me for the first time that bartenders are the hardest to compete with because they're usually funny guys.

I stood there. I decided to really look at everyone. Why not? Why not have a look? I usually went on, did my routine and left without being noticed, so why not have a good gawk? Another hoot from the bar. A waitress with her money apron was in the middle of the room. She had tight blond curls and a friendly face. Her table was laughing at something she'd said. What did she and the bartender have that I didn't?

First, they were familiar. There was nothing I could do about that. Second, they were down there. They were right down there with the customers. The way I had been on the streets.

I lifted the mike out of its stand, then put it back. Forget the mike. I sat down on the edge of the stage. One of the women at the front table turned and looked at me, then went back to her conversation. A few more people looked at me. There was another hoot from the bar. A lot of people at the tables had those frozen smiles on their faces. Every so often they'd burst out into a phony laugh. The hoots from the bar were for real, but something else was going on at the tables.

138

They were acting. Just like at Silvy's parties. I was supposed to be funny for a woman who could laugh uproariously at the guy doing a walrus imitation with two straws up his nose? It reminded me of Lisa and Scott. Lisa, my dorky grade-school friend. Lisa would be good here. She could fake laughter.

A few more people were looking at me. I smiled at them. They looked away. But it was getting quieter at the tables near me. I wasn't going to say anything till it was quiet at the tables. I wouldn't wait for the bar. The bar was another thing entirely.

Someone at the table near the back nodded toward me, and the waitress turned around and looked at me, then she turned back and said something to him. She put down the beers and turned back to me. She had a round tray and she took the money off and put it in her apron, then held the tray in front of her like we used to hold our school books. She put her head on one side and looked at me. I smiled. She smiled. It was suddenly the quietest I'll bet a bar ever gets.

I slid off the stage and I was standing right down on the floor with them, my thighs touching one of the front tables. What was I going to say? *Don't think just start*.

"Then there's the one about the travelling salesman."

They broke up. It was probably a release of tension after having this girl in a sequined vest and tuxedo pants staring at them for five minutes. When it quieted down a voice from the back said, "Are you a stripper or a singer?" The waitress made a motion to bop him on the head but no one

139

noticed her because I was pulling out my vest and looking down at my chest. It went all quiet again.

"A comedian," I said, looking up. That really broke them up. When it quieted down again some guy called out from the bar, "What do we need a comedian for when we got Joe?" The whole bar howled at that. Joe was obviously the bartender.

"Hey, Joe," I called, "get over here." Then the customers picked up on it. They started banging their hands on the tables. "Joe, Joe, Joe, Joe." What could he do? He put down his towel and left the bar. He wouldn't be able to squeeze through, so he went around back and appeared on stage hitching his pants. Everyone applauded, including me. "Take it off!" someone called out, and he did a little bump and grind. They loved it, of course. I held out my hand for Joe to help him down. He hitched his pants again when he was down with me.

"Joe," I said, "what you don't realize is, comedy is very serious business. I'm here to give you a few lessons, Joe." The audience snickered and Joe hitched his pants. I slapped his tummy with the back of my hand. "Suck in your gut, Joe." They laughed. He laughed. "Now, chin up." I tapped under his chin with the back of my hand. "Repeat after me, 'And then there's the airlines.'" The audience hooted. "Go on, Joe, go on." I slapped him under his chin again.

"And then there's the airlines," he said. I looked out at the audience as if to say, "Who is this guy?" A Johnny Carson look. They laughed.

"That's good, Joe, very good. Now, chin up. Chin up and say, 'Anyone here from Moose Jaw?'" The customers went nuts, and a couple of them put up their hands, too. Joe was laughing. "No, no, no, Joe." I squeezed his chubby cheek between my thumb and forefinger. "You mustn't laugh at your own jokes." The lady at the front table got that one. "Now, Joe," I said, facing him. "Be funny."

Joe started to tell a joke about a guy who walks into a bar. Keeping my profile to the audience, I slowly slowly started to nod off. I made it as slow as I possibly could until eventually my forehead was on Joe's shoulder. I waited for the dead quiet moment and when it came, I snored. They hooted and I snapped my head up and yawned and stretched and slapped Joe on the back.

"You're great, Joe. Let's give him a big hand." The audience applauded wildly and he bowed and blew kisses like a true ham. Then when he was climbing back on stage to get off, I pretended to help heave him on. He bowed again and disappeared around the curtain. I knew I had to keep the eyes on me, not on Joe when he emerged heading for the bar.

"Okay, who's next?" There were just laughs and a few people called out other people's names, but no one came up, of course.

"Chickens," I said, making clucking noises. A guy in the front was busting a gut.

"You like that, eh? You like chicken imitations? Gee, this is an easy crowd. Most people want Barbra Streisand but you folks are into barnyard imitations. Okay." I coughed and got them quietened down. I coughed again and looked down as though I was going to do something really hard. I breathed deeply. I waited again for that dead silent moment and when I felt it, I said, "Baaa."

They went nuts. I loved that feeling of getting them all quiet then wild again. Up and down, up and down. After about half an hour of pure improvisation, I worked in a little planned material for fifteen minutes. I could've stayed there forever, but I know you've got to leave them wanting more so I jumped up on the little stage and bowed.

"Thanks, you've been great!" Now I knew why comics always said that at the end of their routines. They *were* great. They were clapping like crazy. What a sound.

TWENTY-FIVE

"**T**HEY want you back." It was Susan's secretary.

"Does Susan know?"

"Not yet. She's in Montreal right now. Can you do it?"

"Sure."

I hung up the phone. They wanted me back! I did a little dance in the hall outside my room. "They want me back," I kept saying out loud. Who could I tell? I dialed Silvy's number.

"Hi, China, is Silvy there?"

"No. I don't know where she is." *Probably reading Brecht with Mark.*

"Is Gina there?"

"I think she's working." *Working on Herbie.* "Sorry, Kim."

"That's okay. I'll call later." I dialed Jeremy. He had a tutorial to teach at two but was free till then, so we met for lunch. Over hamburgers I told him everything in excruciating detail. My visit with Susan, the racket in the club, how I had them going quiet then crazy, quiet then crazy. He wasn't as good at listening to detail as Silvy, but he smiled and said, "You're amazing" a lot. I finally wound down a bit.

"But enough about me, what do *you* think of me?" He laughed.

"I think you're amazing."

"What's amazing is to just let it happen. To not rattle on and on a mile a minute, but just slow down and get right down there with them and let them come to you. There's nothing like it." I suppose if I'd been really attending to Jeremy I'd have seen that his eyes had the same fixed look I felt mine get when *he* talked about world politics. At the time I just thought he was transfixed by my wonderfulness and so I agreed to dinner. A date. A real date with an older man. Jeremy was twenty-one.

I looked wonderful for my date. I wore a dress I'd bought at Ex-Toggery because I couldn't resist it but had never worn yet. It was dead simple. A teal blue tank top dress that hung straight on me, and I wore it with skinny flat sandals and the enormous hoop earrings I'd bought on my last shopping spree with Skye. Jeremy had never seen me in anything but T's and sneaks or my vest and tuxedo pants. He was suitably stunned.

"You like my dress?"

"It's . . . amazing."

I usually walked through the laundromat unnoticed, but this time a couple of women just watched me the whole time while they kept folding laundry. Get used to it, I thought. When you're famous they'll be staring at you like this all the time. Jeremy had borrowed his roommate's car. I felt so grown up and worldly wise. He kept glancing over at me but I pretended not to notice.

Once we were sitting in the restaurant, Jeremy said, "You have amazing hair." I'd bent over and brushed it, then spritzed it to keep the volume. And I'd lined my eyes with kohl the way Skye and I used to do. The way Silvy did before Mark.

The waiter turned up and asked if we wanted a drink. Obviously *he* couldn't tell I was almost but not quite eighteen.

144

"I'll just have a glass of white wine," I said. I was determined not to be excited or jerky tonight but fluid and elegant. Katharine Hepburn all the way. Jeremy ordered us a small carafe of white wine. He was just looking at me. At least he wasn't rambling on and on about Russia. There was a lull in the conversation.

"Have you always wanted to do this?"

"What, comedy? No. I never really wanted to do it. It just happened."

"You're kidding."

"No. I wanted, want, to be an actor."

"Like Silvy."

"Well, yeah." I didn't want to say so, but I wanted to be in the movies, not weird plays at midnight with only twenty people in the audience. "Anyway, this is what's happening now so this is what I'll do. For now."

"I could never be that . . . flexible." Jeremy said. "I have to know what I'm going to be doing from day to day. Year to year."

"Decade to decade?" He laughed.

"Ideally, yeah." I tried to smile an indulgent smile, but inside I was thinking *how boring*.

But I was not going to let the fact that Jeremy and I were from different planets spoil a potentially lovely evening. Neither was he. During dinner — steak and salad for my companion, fettuccine alfredo pour moi — we tried to find something to talk about other than politics or my triumphant club date. It was hard, but eventually we found old movies. The problem was he always wanted to talk about the political daring of Charlie Chaplin's "Little Tramp," and I always wanted to talk about Chaplin's timing. Over dessert and

145

coffee we smiled a lot. I had a game that Skye and Silvy had both been great at. You pick someone at a table and make up a life and a story for them, but I didn't try it out on Jeremy. Not because I thought it would seem too childish — because I figured I could pull off a Katharine Hepburn kind of charm with it — but because I didn't think he'd be any good at it. Some games take two.

When the bill came I snuck a look at it. Fifty-two dollars and ninety-five cents. Sheesh. This made me feel warmly toward Jeremy again, so I didn't say anything when he put his hand on my back to guide me out of the restaurant, although it gave me the creeps. He was probably just playing someone else, too. Not Leslie Howard or Errol Flynn, though. Probably his dad.

We didn't say much on the drive home. When he pulled up in front of the laundromat and turned off the ignition I knew he was going to walk me to the door so I asked if he wanted to come in for coffee. He said yes. He looked uncomfortable sitting on my vinyl chair, but then Jeremy looked uncomfortable everywhere. I felt sorry for him. There he was twenty-one with facial hair and he looked like a goof. I felt like a woman of the world. After all, I spent my nights handling drunks.

"Nice room."

"It's small but I love it," I said, handing him a coffee and trying to lounge, not perch, on the bed. "Not bad for seventeen." He started to choke on his coffee so badly that I got up and whacked him on the back.

"You okay?"

"Fine," he spluttered, "fine. You're only seventeen?" I was about to say "almost eighteen" when

146

he grabbed me and kissed me. He pressed his chin into mine so hard the whiskers hurt. I figured this was passion and I figured it was time for me to fake that, too. I kissed him back. As Jeremy manoeuvred me backward toward my little single bed, all I could think of was, "Now I'll have two things to tell Silvy when I see her."

TWENTY-SIX

"WHAT have you done to your hair?"
"I dyed it back to its original colour."
"Brown?"
"Yeah. Don't you like it?"
"What's not to like, or like, about brown?"
"Thanks a lot." I couldn't believe Silvy had dyed her beautiful pink hair brown.

"This is for Mark, right? The John Lennon clone." I made A-OK signs of my thumbs and fingers and held them up to my eyes for hostile glasses. And I started to sing. IMAGINE ALL THE PEE-PUH-UH-UL, LIVING IN HARMONY, UH OH OH OH. Silvy was laughing even though I was ribbing her man.

"Kim, you're dreadful."

"Dreadful? *Dread*ful? Help! My friend has been possessed by Princess Di! Help!" We were sitting on a bench in a parkette. Not a frisbee paused in flight. "Look at them. Possession doesn't frighten them."

"Well, not by Princess Di, anyway. Satan, maybe."

"Good point. So this is the new old you, eh?"
"Um-hm."

"And you're doing it for yourself, not Mark?" She looked up at the sky.

"'But love, fair looks, and true obedience; Too little payment for so great a debt.'"

"Say, what?"

"Shakespeare."

"You're going to be in a Shakespeare play?"

148

"No. I'm just reading it."

"You're reading Shakespeare? When you don't have to?"

"Yes." I took her pulse and felt her head.

"We're losing her. Start the epibumthum drip. Stat."

"I'm allergic to epibumthum."

"No, you're not."

"Yes, I am."

"Noyou'renot."

"YesIam!"

"Oh, Silvy," I sighed. "You're slipping away from me." I was actually serious now. "You're going to start walking around spouting Shakespeare and wearing drab clothes and you won't want anything to do with your friend, Flame."

"Don't be stupid. People have to change and move on. Look how much you've changed in a year. You've gone from mild-mannered street performer to cabaret star." I'd told her about my triumph on the phone. I couldn't wait. But I hadn't told her about Jeremy yet. "And I'll always want to see my friend Flame."

"I'll be an embarrassment to you. You'll be the star of alternative theatre and I'll be this clown in your past."

"Will you cut it out? You know, sometimes I can't tell when you're serious and when you're joking."

"That's the way I like it."

"Well, it's maddening." I buried my head in my hands.

"Oh, God, you see, it's started." I grabbed her arm and put the back of my other hand to my

forehead. "GOODBYE. COUGH, COUGH, REMEM-
BER ME, COUGH, WITH KINDNESS."

"Kim?"

"Hm?"

"Tell me all about Jeremy."

"Ah, yes, Jeremy. The old Silvy would have been more interested in hearing about my craft."

"I heard all about your craft for an hour this morning on the phone."

"Only an hour? I must have left something out."

"Probably. So tell me about Jeremy. Did you sleep together?"

"Yes."

"What? Really? Last night?"

"Last night."

"That's fantastic! Well, it's about time."

What I didn't tell Silvy and had no intention of telling Silvy was that we had done just that. Sleep together. Jeremy was very embarrassed about it and I was very relieved and we slept together in my skinny little bed and that morning I had pretended to be fast asleep while he got into his shoes and jacket and slipped out. He left me a note on a U of T memo pad that said:

Thank you for a lovely evening.
                              Jeremy.

Unfortunately, I was on my way to the bathroom when a flustered Jeremy came back upstairs to use the pay phone in the hall.

"My car's been towed!" he said. This part of the story I told Silvy.

"Poor Jeremy."

"Poor Jeremy. It was his friend's car, too. Cost

150

him fifty-four dollars and a couple of missed classes."

"Never mind. He had a nice evening."

Poor Jeremy. I'd stayed in the bathroom awhile but I couldn't stay there too long without it looking like I was avoiding him. I wished I'd stayed in bed pretending to be asleep a little longer and I could have avoided seeing him at all that morning. When he got off the phone I was standing there.

"Well." He looked at the memo pad where he'd written the address of the towing company and the price. "I guess I know what I'm doing this morning."

"Guess so." Jeremy brought new meaning to the words "awkward silence."

"May I see you again?" *I'd rather not.*

"Of course. I'd like that."

"Really?" *No.*

"Really."

He gave me a whiskery dry little kiss and went off searching for his roommate's car. I went back to my room and lay on top of my bed until I figured it was late enough to call Silvy. I would never call a theatre person before noon.

"Gee," Silvy said, taking my chin in her hand and looking at me head on, then in profile. "You don't look any different." I shrugged.

"It's no big deal."

"See? That's what I told you. Now you'll stop mooning over that Brad guy." *Oh, no, I won't.* "And now you've got to get pills."

"What?" I didn't want to think about any of this. Besides, nothing had actually happened.

"You can come see my doctor. She's really nice. Almost human. She's got a nose ring."

151

"You're kidding."

"Nope."

"Okay."

I decided to go along with Silvy because I knew that even if nothing happened with Jeremy, it was bound to sometime and I'd better be prepared. It sure wasn't romantic, though. It seemed so calculated.

The doctor was nice. The nose ring wasn't too much to get excited about, just a flat little gold disk. Maybe she put a ruby in for her nights out. She gave me a bunch of samples for free when I told her I was a comedian. I don't carry a purse so I gave them to Silvy who was waiting for me. There were a lot of teenagers in the waiting room. I guessed that was her specialty.

"You don't have to look like you just lost your best friend," Silvy said as we walked down the long carpeted hall to the elevator. But I felt like I had lost my best friend. My fantasy. No more chance of a moonlit terrace, no buttons.

Sex. What a concept.

TWENTY-SEVEN

SUSAN was very pleased about the repeat work I was getting, but by the time she heard I'd already told everybody so my excitement had died down a bit. She seemed to think it was her little pep talk that did the trick. Probably it was. I figured she knew what she was doing and I'd better listen to her. I'd totally given up my fantasy of her as a motherly type wrapping her arms around me and telling me how wonderful I was.

She got me a club date in Humbletown, so I decided to combine it with an eighteenth birthday party visit to the old homestead. Big mistake. Dad sat across from me at the table. Little Ronnie was on his lap slobbering. He sure loved the little guy. And he and Ron had never got along so well. Weird. Dad was looking at me strangely.

"Well, Kim, what's your decision?" I just looked at him. "You've had your year. Are you coming home?" I was stunned. Kathy was the first one to speak.

"Dad, she's doing really well. Why would she come home?"

"Thanks, Kathy," I said. Debbie looked really nervous. As though she might have to watch a family fight. I didn't feel like fighting. I felt like crying.

"But," my mother said, "how long can you go on like this? Playing in these clubs?" To my horror I found myself spouting Susan's lines.

"Listen, Jay Leno still does two hundred and fifty one-nighters a year. *This* is not some degrading thing, *this* is what it's all about. It's what the big guys are doing."

"It doesn't sound like much of a life."

I knew my voice was going to get teenybopper screechy, but I couldn't help myself.

"You're the one who always told me I could do anything!"

"But this?" She said *this* as though I was hooking or something.

"You don't even know what *this* is! You've never come to see me. Ever."

Debbie, in her quiet little voice, said, "I'll stay with Ronnie, Gloria, and you can go see Kim." *Yes. Yes! Come see me, Mum.*

"No, honey, you need a break. I'll stay with Ronnie." I stood up.

"I'm going to the club. I don't care if no one comes."

I didn't want to stand outside the house for the Locke Street bus, so I walked up Dundurn to King Street. I was mad. I was mad because I'd behaved like a kid instead of a grownup. *I don't care if no one comes.* Sheesh. They were probably all carrying on about how much I'd changed. Didn't they realize I was earning money as a comic? Everyone else in my life thought that was pretty amazing.

I got on the bus. I didn't have exact change so I had to stuff two dollars in. I didn't care. When I plunked down in the front seat you're supposed to leave for old folks, it hit me. Ron was doing exactly what Dad had done! Get married, get a job at Stelco, have a baby. Only the order had changed. No wonder they were getting along better these days. Like father like son. Well, I didn't want to work for a lawyer and have babies.

154

I got off the bus early so I could walk off a little steam before I got to the club. There were the usual million crows in front of City Hall. Those crows drove me nuts. City Hall with its stupid football sculpture drove me nuts. The old feeling of being fed up with Humbletown was welling up inside me. All the memories of being a dork at Ryerson, overshadowed by Skye at Westdale, betrayed by Brad, all came flooding back. I was getting angry.

I'd performed sad and I'd performed happy, but I'd never really performed angry.

"Ladies and gentlemen, let's give a warm welcome to Kimberly Taylor!"

"You call that warm? I call that pathetic! C'mon, try again. Better. Much better. *Where are Ron and Kathy and Debbie? In the middle there. Not up front, not in the back, smack in the middle.* "I used to live in Hamilton, The Ambitious City. I know the Jolley Cut is not a new way to slice roast beef." *Chuckles. Mere chuckes.* "But the streets do all go the wrong way." *These people are dead.* "Okay. Let's try another topic. Money. Money is something dear to all our hearts, right?" *Dead.* "My mother read somewhere once that to raise a kid costs one hundred and fifty thousand dollars. I tried to explain to her that this depended on many things — not the least of which was *having* a hundred and fifty thousand dollars — like, fancy schools and riding lessons. But she wouldn't listen to me. YOU'RE NOT COSTING *ME* A HUNDRED AND FIFTY THOUSAND DOLLARS, she'd say. I'd be on my way to have a bath. A BATH? AGAIN? YOU'RE NOT COSTING *ME* A HUNDRED AND FIFTY THOU-

155

SAND DOLLARS, YOUNG LADY. Notice how you're Young Lady in these situations?" *My God, not a laugh. And Ron's looking at me like*, Mum never said that. *Sheesh*. "I smell formaldehyde, folks. Get it? Embalmed? Dead, you see."

"You're not funny, sweetie."

Oh, great. A joker. I could zap him between the eyes, but Kathy and Debbie would be embarrassed. I'll just keep going.

"Anyway, mothers have their own logic, don't they? It's that LOOK AT ME WHEN I'M TALKING TO YOU DON'T LOOK AT ME LIKE THAT kind of logic. It makes sense to them."

"Hey, sweetie." *Oh, no. This guy's going to keep repeating himself till I bite.* "You're not funny." *Right again, Kim.*

"Funny. I'm not your sweetie, either. *Well, that didn't get much of a laugh. This is a nervous crowd.* The other day I was shopping at Eaton's — "

"I wouldn't want a sweetie with a honker like that."

Okay. Okay, Kim. The guy's drunk. Ignore him or handle him gently. Do not try to top him.

I can't help it. Comedy makes you mean.

"*You* have a *sweetie*?"

Now he puts his arm around a woman's shoulders. She gives everyone a big smile as though she's proud of the jerk. I should let them get on with it, but I have a lot of anger built up from before the show.

"Whatever he's paying you, honey, it's not worth it."

My initial reaction is pleasure at having scored a point, because the crowd roars. My next reaction is fear because the guy removes his arm from his

156

"sweetie" as though he's going to get up. My third reaction is regret because of my brother and sister. They look terrified.

I decide to try a trick I've got up my sleeve but never had to use before. I pull a white hanky from my pocket and wave it in surrender. It seems to work. The beefy guy sits there scowling, and his girlfriend looks at me with her mouth hanging open. Hang on, Kim. You can get through this. Do your Queen's Christmas Speech. It's a guaranteed crowd-pleaser.

"Hellow, and melly Chrrristmas . . ." *Oh, nice. Very nice. Beefcake and Bimbo have decided the way to save face is to talk to each other as though I'm not here.* "My husband and ayey . . ." *Right. This is making an already nervous crowd very very nervous. I have to do something. I'll clap my hands. That got their attention.* "Okay, kids, that's enough. Go to your rooms." *I don't believe this! The jerk is actually giving me the finger.* "That's original. You learned that from her, right?"

Now, this guy's particularly abusive, but I've dealt with his kind before. The problem is, with Ron and Kathy and Debbie here, I'm a lot more hesitant. So when he comes up with his next line I don't top him.

"Whatsa matter?" Beefcake says, his hands on his knees as though he's getting ready to stand. "Put your tampon in backwards?"

Ron isn't hesitant at all. He lunges at the guy. Debbie screams his name, but it's no good. He's on top of my heckler. Beefy's girlfriend tries to hit Ron with her purse. Then it happens. With the most awful sound I've ever heard, Beefy hauls off and punches Ron in the face. Ron falls backwards and Debbie runs to him and a couple of guys try to grab Beefcake by the arms.

So here I am in Yuk Yuks, site of my first professional triumph, and my worst nightmare has come true. Fighting in the aisles. Blood and gore. My very own brother's blood. My very own brother's gore. I can see the headlines: ASPIRING COMIC'S BROTHER BEATEN TO PULP IN BAR ROOM BRAWL. Susan will like that. Publicity.

Mum and Dad won't. They'll give me those dinnertime looks and shake their heads. "Is it worth it, Kim?" they'll say. "This crazy life you lead. Is it worth *this*?"

They don't know the half of it. Coaxing laughs out of strangers, never having enough money, never knowing what your next job is or whether they'll like you or hate you. They don't know the *half* of it. But I know what my answer will be. Even as I watch my brother getting dragged away by his armpits, his face covered in blood.

"Yeah. It is. It's worth it."

Also by Mitzi Dale

Round the Bend

Everyone thinks Deirdre's crazy. But she doesn't
agree. After all, what's so crazy about daydreaming
every chance you get, or noticing just how weird
adults can be, or screaming your head off when
you realize your mother is reading magazine
articles to figure you out? But when she sets fire to
her bed, even Deirdre has to admit something's
wrong.

Shunted from psychiatrist to hospital to group
home, Deirdre struggles to make her way back to
the real world, through the friendship of a nine-year-
old kleptomaniac and comic book addict and with
the help of an off-the-wall therapist.

ISBN 0-88899-069-3

The Sky's the Limit

More than anything, Kim wants to leave her
steelworking town behind and break into showbiz.
Her dream is to be a standup comic, and she
spends hours in front of a full-length mirror
perfecting her routines—Amy the Baton-twirling
Typical Teen, Shy Shirley, and the Adolescent
Male.

But first there are four years of high school to get
through—four years that will be sheer hell unless
she can avoid being labelled a loser. So while her
friends decide that the only way to be cool is to
snare a boyfriend—any boyfriend—Kim decides on
another strategy. She plots to befriend the most
popular girl in school. Skye Manning is beautiful,
accomplished, rich and talented. Skye, it seems,
has absolutely everything a girl could want . . .

ISBN 0-88899-121-5